D0436757

ALSO BY URSULA HEGI

The Worst Thing I've Done

Sacred Time

Hotel of the Saints

The Vision of Emma Blau

Tearing the Silence

Salt Dancers

Stones from the River

Floating in My Mother's Palm

Unearned Pleasures and Other Stories

Intrusions

Trudi & Pia

Children and Fire

A Novel

Ursula Hegi

Scribner
New York London Toronto Sydney

SCRIBNER
A Division of Simon & Schuster, Inc.
1230 Avenue of the Americas
New York, NY 10020

First Scribner hardcover edition May 2011

Book design by Ellen R. Sasahara

Manufactured in the United States of America

10 9 8 7 6 5 4 3 2 1

Library of Congress Cataloging-in-Publication Data is available.

ISBN 978-1-4516-0829-8
ISBN 978-1-4516-0831-1 (ebook)

For Adam, Cheri, and Aaron

Acknowledgments

I THANK MY EDITOR Mark Gompertz and my agents Gail Hochman and Marianne Merola for—once again—taking this journey with me. Many thanks to Gordon Gagliano, Rod Stackelberg, Lou Ann Walker, and Barbara Wright, who read drafts of this novel and offered their valuable insights. In my research, I learned much from the works of Erika Mann, Alexander Bahar, Wilfried Kugel, and William H. Allen.

Contents

Tuesday, February 27, 1934

Chapter 1

A WINTER MORNING IN 1934. Imagine frost on the windowpanes of the schoolhouse in this village by the Rhein, milk blossoms of frost. Imagine the chill on the necks of the boys in Fräulein Jansen's classroom. Feel their dread because today is the first anniversary of the fire that destroyed the parliament building in Berlin, a fire that has scorched their dreams in a whoosh of yellow and red, jagged and fast, so fast it's like a whip, like a hot wind, clutching at timbers till they cave in.

"What if the communists burn our school?" the boys ask their young teacher.

"Will they attack our village?"

"Oh no." She tries to calm them. "The fire happened far away from here. Hundreds of kilometers."

But the boys have heard about the fire so often that they're frightened it will happen here in Burgdorf. They've heard about it on the people's radio and in their parents' discussions over who really burned down the parliament building. Most parents repeat what's on the radio, that the communists set the fire. But other parents whisper that the Nazis set the fire to frame the communists.

"We are safe here," the teacher promises her boys. And hopes it's true.

*

They want to believe her. Because they adore her. Because she makes them feel proud. Because she gets them to laugh till their belly muscles ache. Because—and this they don't know but will figure out as men, those who'll survive the next war—she keeps the shutters open at night, even in winter, to feel moon on her skin. It takes a certain kind of teacher to do this, one who leaps and runs with her boys when she takes them outdoors.

"What if the communists burn my barn, Fräulein Jansen?"

"What if they blow up our bridges?" Otto's voice is fearful.

But some of her boys look excited.

Thekla Jansen knows why. As a girl, she built bonfires with her Catholic youth group. The girls and their leader would sit around the flames, roasting potatoes and competing with stories about creatures that arose from the underbellies of their dreams. In the mist—stories like that are always more exciting in the mist—the girls would huddle closer, shout with delicious fear, lure the beast inside their circle of flames, and laugh at it till it faded away.

Andreas raises his hand. "The communists sleep on steel floors, not in beds, that's how tough they are."

"We have three cows, and if we can't get them out—"

"What if they sink our ferry?"

"Five cows. We have five."

The teacher rests one hand on the piano, against the glass frog house where Icarus lives. The frog's heartbeat pulsates on every surface of his body, flashy and rapid, as if his body were his heart. Icarus survives on the dead flies the boys peel off sticky coils of flypaper that dangle from their kitchen ceilings.

"I was afraid, too," Thekla Jansen says. "Especially those nights after the Reichstag burned."

*

Startled that their teacher is admitting to fear, her boys lean forward in the wooden rows of desks, two to each row. Most of her ten-year-olds are already in uniform, pins of the new flag on their brown collars. But the nine-year-olds, too young to join, wear threadbare shirts buttoned to their throats, borders of white collar only on those boys who own their schoolbooks; for the poor boys, it's one book shared by two.

"For weeks I kept checking for flames and smoke above our roofs," she says and wonders if her boys, too, will forever remember where they were when they found out.

For her it was at a costume ball, dancing with friends from her university days to music from an orchestra of clowns. *Rosenmontag*—Shrove Monday, the pomp and glory of parades and floats and music and masks, your last fling because once Lent began, you had to atone for your sins and mistakes. *Rosenmontag,* the next to last day of *Karneval,* when all of Germany let loose in frivolity, when—behind your mask—you could be anyone you chose. As Thekla danced in the red and black flamenco costume her mother, Almut, had sewn, words shattered the music, a man's voice from the *Volksempfänger*—people's radio saying the Reichstag was on fire in Berlin, saying it as though he didn't believe it, his voice urgent and climbing like the highest note of music itself. The costumed dancers froze as if in a pantomime as the voice described how, there in Berlin, ghosts and jesters and Vikings and Chinamen and ballerinas and prophets and Indians and angels and cats and Dutch girls with wooden clogs were swarming from restaurants and bars toward the blazing cupola of the Reichstag, while men in uniform, firefighters and SA and police, tried to block the bizarre witnesses from getting too close.

*

"Do you remember where you were when you heard about the Reichstag fire?" Thekla Jansen asks her students.

A murmur. A hum. Several hands rising.

"I was allowed to stay up late because of *Rosenmontag*. A neighbor came in and told us."

"I heard on the radio."

"I went to sleep in my costume."

"I was a cowboy with—"

"I was a Chinaman. My *Oma* made me a yellow hat that's like an umbrella."

"—with two holsters and a mustache."

"My mother woke me up and took me outside," Richard says. "Some houses were dark. She kept wondering who knew about the fire. And who didn't."

"Did you have a mask, Fräulein?"

"Black satin with red stones." Thekla remembers how troubled she felt as she pulled off her mask, and again on *Aschermittwoch*—Ash Wednesday two days later, when the priest's thumb drew the cross of ash on the forehead of each parishioner. The scent of ashes in his golden bowl tilted her back into the night of ashes falling on Berlin—*Ashes to ashes. To whom must I answer?*—as though the Reichstag fire had been the harbinger for this ash on her skin; and she envisioned future Ash Wednesdays, years funneling into decades, when the cool smudge on her forehead would summon that fire for her.

"It started fourteen minutes past nine," says Franz. Pants too short, but quick with numbers.

"I was asleep. But my father told me the next morning and said it would be a different world tomorrow."

"My mother said anything can happen now, and that we must stock up on food that can't spoil."

"We bought lentils and peas."

"My father, he was yelling," Bruno Stosick says. He's the son of the teacher's landlord, a brainy child who can recite every move of historic chess games but doesn't know how to play in the dirt. Already, Bruno is a chess champion, has grown up within the Burgdorf Chess Club that meets every Tuesday in his family's living room.

Soon after the teacher rented the apartment above the chess club, Bruno began sneaking up the steps in his socks to play his hiding games. He'd knock at her door, hide behind the coatrack in the hallway. When she'd open her door and pretend to be surprised nobody was there, he'd leap out, smelling of chalk and of sleep, tip his face to her—"I thought you'd never find me!"—such sweetness in his smile, it's almost too much for a boy.

But Bruno isn't smiling now. He's imitating his father's hoarse voice: "'Everyone knows that damn Austrian started the fire!'"

Most of the students giggle.

But some don't.

Bruno digs his fingernails into his palms. "My father says the Führer should be strung up by his—"

"Bruno!" Alarmed, the teacher cuts him off. She has never seen him like this. "We do not say swear words."

As if 'damn' mattered one damn to me. But this is what she wants her boys to recall when they tell their group leaders or their parents about school: that their teacher scolded Bruno Stosick for saying *damn*—and not that Bruno's father wants the Führer strung up by his balls. Or, rather, by his one and only ball. If rumors are to be trusted.

Chapter 2

BOYS," SHE SAYS, "please repeat after me: We. Do. Not. Say. Swear. Words."

They recite: "We. Do. Not. Say. Swear. Words."

Not enough. She needs more from them to undo what Bruno said. Folding her hands, she nods toward the portrait of the Führer above the piano, where the crucifix used to be. "And now a prayer for the Führer."

By order, all crucifixes have been removed from schools; yet, prayer has remained. As long as it's for him. That homely man with his prissy mustache.

—*Nein nein jetzt nicht. Weg damit*—No no not now. Away with this—

Appalling, how much her boys expose about their families in all innocence. She would never turn them in. Still, others might.

Especially since last Tuesday's faculty meeting, when Sister Mäuschen suggested essays about dinner conversations. *Mäuschen.* Little Mouse. A nickname the sister had been given as a child.

There must have been a birth name before that, a saint's name—there always was—because there certainly was no saint named Little Mouse.

"To help us identify families that are not supportive of the Führer," Sister Mäuschen said.

The school nurse, Sister Agathe, quickly shook her head. The students liked her because she gave them licorice and told them riddles.

Nearly everyone in that meeting looked at the principal, Sister Josefine, who was passionate about learning, who advocated that all children were born with the impulse to create things that were not there before—pictures and stories and songs—and that out of that impulse came wanting to learn more. Sister Josefine had finesse, and she used that finesse to procure whatever her school needed: radios and teachers and books and repairs. For herself, she craved poverty. Spartan self-discipline. She was accustomed to obedience—the obedience of others—because she'd grown up on an estate with horses and tutors and servants.

For the sake of her school, she'd offer up any student or teacher who might cause conflict. Nuns whispered that Sister Josefine tangoed with the government, wrapped it into her virgin-nun dance. Still, they had faith she'd calculate just how much they must let the government lead so they wouldn't risk losing their convent and their school.

But Sister Josefine said nothing to contradict Sister Mäuschen.

*

If Thekla could advise the Führer what to change—just one change if he were to ask her, one single change—she would remind him of his promise to strengthen the German family, get him to understand that children denouncing their parents weakened the family.

While her boys pray, Thekla decides she must warn Bruno's parents, not only about what he revealed in class, but also about him climbing from his window to go to rallies. Tonight. Tonight she will tell his parents.

Last fall, when Thekla's mother told her the Stosicks' rental was vacant, Thekla went to see it: parquet floors, tall windows, a bathtub deeper than that of the Abramowitz family, for whom her mother worked as the housekeeper.

When Herr Stosick quoted her the rent, Thekla confessed she'd estimated it to be twice that much.

"An honor to have you live here," he said. "A colleague, after all."

Gisela Stosick nodded. As usual, she was all of one color—sandy dress, sandy scarf, sandy hair—except for her shoes, top-stitched leather in two shades of blue. Gisela liked flamboyant shoes.

"It'll be good for our Bruno," she told Thekla, "to get to know his teacher."

Thekla was astonished how welcoming Gisela was. As girls they'd been classmates and in the same youth group, but once Gisela had married, she'd set herself above her unmarried friends.

*

How to talk to the Stosicks without betraying Bruno's trust? If they weren't so strict, he wouldn't need to come to Thekla with his secrets. Like joining the Hitler-Jugend last December, as soon as he could after his tenth birthday. For him it was different than for her other boys, who felt like adults once they joined, important. Bruno had been a little adult all his life, *altklug*—old-wise, competing with his mind; but once he belonged to the Hitler-Jugend, he got to compete with his body, and discovered the joy of exertion as he leapt and ran, trained for distance and speed, proved himself as part of this sprawling team that included and absorbed him.

But within two weeks, his parents found out and forbade him to belong.

Now they won't let him out of the house alone. It mortifies Bruno when his mother walks him to and from school as if he were a little boy.

Early this morning the teacher heard him crying downstairs; then his father's voice, firm; his father's steps, heavy, in the bathroom. Herr Stosick takes up more space than his wife and son together. The click of the dog's toenails on the kitchen floor, then scratching at the back door. Soon, the dog's dance with the door, throwing herself at it, wailing, scratching, until someone let Henrietta out. Some mornings Thekla used to hear laughter downstairs. But not lately. Bruno has been sullen. Agitated.

So many losses for him.

The comradery of the Hitler-Jugend.

His best friend, Markus Bachmann. Markus, who murmured instructions to himself whenever he sketched because he already envisioned the finished piece. Who hiccuped when he laughed. Who was always rushing himself, though he was one of the brightest boys in Thekla's class. Markus had two best friends, Otto and Bruno, but Bruno had only Markus as a friend. And now he's too alone in her classroom.

Two Jewish families have left Burgdorf so far. The Gutbergs last December on a flight to London. A few weeks later Markus's family on a ship to America. So unsettling, Thekla thinks, that heat against the Jews, people saying that their greed caused inflation and unemployment, that they came from nowhere and were taking over everything. On the radio it often was: communists and Jews, as if they were the same. Even at St. Martin's Church, some parishioners make unkind remarks about Jews. Of course, Thekla never agrees, talks about something else, if she can.

*

When she followed Bruno to the rally, she could spot right away that it had been organized by people who understood about teaching, how to respect children and inspire them. It was the way Thekla taught, instinctively.

Too many of her students had been raised with the rule that children should be seen but not heard. Of course it was intoxicating for them now to have a voice, to be told they were important, Germany's future. Alone, none of these children had power; yet, being part of the marching columns gave them a mysterious power, all of them moving as one. That part made Thekla uneasy, and she wouldn't mind saying that to Bruno's parents.

But what she wouldn't admit to them is how, from being critical one moment, she was sucked into the swirl of song and of fire, into the emotions of the mass, that passion and urgency, that longing for something beyond them, something great, till she could no longer separate herself, till those emotions became hers, too, that hand to her throat, that sigh, that upsweep of her arm. She felt repulsed. But she didn't let herself show it. Because someone might be watching. Because it might be a trap. And because just before that moment of repulsion—for the duration of a single heartbeat—she had felt the children's rapture as her own, felt their pride at being part of this ceremony that was as mystical as church and as lavish as opera with its pomp and music and processions.

*

It was like some crush, some moony devotion, when you lose all hold on yourself and can no longer be responsible. *Where am I? Where have I gone to? What if it will be like this from now on?* She didn't want that feeling, just as she didn't like falling in love. *Because of what you give up.* Loving was different. It was only the falling she minded. She wished she could love like a man, be skin only, lust only. Her friend, Emil, was good practice. With a man like Emil Hesping, you didn't need to worry about breaking his heart. It was known in Burgdorf that he got away from any woman unlucky enough to fall for him. Still, women of all ages were drawn to his genuine liking of them, to his curiosity about the minute details of their lives, to his energy that he focused so totally on each of them. With a man like Emil, a woman might be tempted to tame him so that he would adore her, only her. But not a single one could hold him for long—though he might return to her, for a while—not even the milliner, Frau Simon, so flamboyant with her laugh and her red hair.

Whenever Thekla danced with him, his touch was fast bliss throughout her body. Even when they linked arms on their walks. It was the strongest response she'd had to any man. More like an allergy. So far, she had not slept with Emil. Not because it might lessen his pursuit. And not because of the church. That, she had sorted out with her conscience when she was nineteen and had her first lover, dismissing chastity with its inherent guilt. Just as she dismissed the story of God creating the world in six days. And yet, she liked the rituals of mass and redemption. On the first Saturday of each month, she knelt in the half-dark of the confessional and revealed to the priest her so-called immoral thoughts and acts, counting on him to absolve her, bless her, restore her virginity in the eyes of God, a joke and a miracle.

She hadn't slept with Emil because for her sex skidded into longing, into that moony falling that made her afraid of losing the beloved though she had no intention of marrying him, or anyone. Living with two brothers had shown her how much marriage took from women. For herself, she wanted Emil's impermanence. Soon, she would leave him. Because of his reputation. Not with women. But with politics. Until the burning of the Reichstag, she, too, had made fun of Nazis—that they couldn't add without counting fingers; that their Führer bit into carpets when he got furious—but ridiculing them was no longer safe.

*

When the rally ended, she waited for Bruno without letting him see her. She told herself it had just been pageantry that appealed to small-town minds conditioned by religion to narrow ranges of pleasure. It was probably of value to her teaching to have felt what an adventure it was for her boys to be one with this mass that marched and sang. Passion came into it. The sacred. The ancient. Pride. And now that was over. Until the next time. And she didn't have to think about it till then.

As she followed Bruno through the dark streets, she felt a terrible foreboding because he looked so small, almost indistinguishable from the walls that seemed to slant toward him as if to collapse.

She called out his name.

Startled, he turned.

"I don't want you out alone at night," she whispered. "I was at the rally and—"

He got so happy that he cried, going on about how he loved the Führer and the rally and his uniform.

"Sshhh . . ." She glanced around, brought her index finger to his lips to calm him. "You're tired."

"Now I know what it's like to live." He could be so pompous.

"Oh, Bruno. I want you to promise me something."

"Yes."

"I want you to wake me up if you plan to climb from your window again."

"But—"

"So that I can go with you. As long as one adult is with you . . ." She didn't know how to end her sentence. Couldn't promise him that his parents, in time, would let him belong.

Still, he promised to wake her.

Chapter 3

WHEN THE PRAYER ends in Fräulein Jansen's classroom, the only sound is that of pigeons scratching at the frozen dirt in the flower box that the boys and their teacher built last May and attached to the brick ledge outside their window. They planted flowers to attract butterflies: *Gänseblümchen*—daisies and *Lavendel* and *Ringelblumen*—marigold.

Thekla used to buy corn for the street pigeons whenever she could afford it, but now, with her teacher's salary, she can every week. Can afford to buy decent food for herself and give money to *Mutti,* who does Thekla's laundry. Across her dresser, she has spread the table runner *Mutti* embroidered for her. Almut Jansen's embroidery is treasured in Burgdorf, and she sells it at the Christmas market. She also barters it for groceries from Weiler's store, books from the pay-library, and medical advice from Frau Doktor Rosen.

Franz raises his hand. "How many kilometers to Berlin, Fräulein?"

What her boys need from her right now is a lesson in geography—not the lesson about Lent she's supposed to teach. She's always willing to abandon her curriculum, teach instead what her boys want to find out that very moment, and it's then that she feels her connection to them most deeply.

"Identifying our students' enthusiasm is half of our teaching," her favorite teacher used to say. Fräulein Siderova taught every day as if it were her first, with that readiness for wonder and discovery. That's how Thekla wants her boys to experience learning—through touch and memory. Once the knowledge is inside them, she can deepen it, let it support future knowledge.

"Who can tell us how many kilometers to Berlin?" she asks. Granted, this will be geography via fear, but it'll calm her boys and teach them to remember where Berlin is.

"Is it over three hundred?"

"Over two hundred?"

A storm of hands, up, more enthusiasm than she can expect during her lesson on Lent. To lecture about Lent may be appropriate when there is plenty of food; but with such poverty in the country, it would be cruel to influence children to give up anything else. She's seen devastating poverty when she's visited some of her boys' families; and yet, their mothers will offer her food they cannot spare. "I just ate," Thekla will lie, even if she feels hungry, her saliva slick in her throat. She understands the shame of being poor, not letting on that your furniture is being repossessed, pretending you don't witness your neighbors' disgrace. *Pretending—*

*

She loves them all: the boys with crossed eyes and the boys with crooked teeth; the brainy boys and the beautiful boys; the boys from good families and the boys with *Rotznasen*—runny noses—who've been born into families where something as basic as wiping your nose is not done for you when you're little, and you never learn how to do it for yourself. Like the Führer. This is where he came from, and the uniform can't cover that. His skin may be clean and dry, but he'll always have that *Rotznase*. It's a way of living, a way of having been brought into life.

At least my boys are thriving in school, Thekla reminds herself. At least they're not as thin anymore. They've become more playful, mischievous, chasing each other with chalkboard erasers . . . gluing her chair to the floor . . . and she'll play along by pretending to be exasperated.

She smiles at Franz, whose *Vater,* after three years of unemployment, is working at the bakery, though only in the dawn hours; at Eckart, whose *Mutter* is finally back at her job cleaning St. Martin's Church; at Otto, whose father repairs sewing machines in Düsseldorf.

"Our lives are getting better, right?" she asks.

Only Otto nods.

To reassure the others, she adds, "Remember, the Führer promised on the radio that he'll make the world safer." She doesn't let on how she resents his grating voice whenever it interrupts her teaching.

In the principal's office the *Volksempfänger* is on constantly. Loudspeakers, once used for prayers, now alert nuns and teachers to listen with their students whenever the Führer gives yet another speech. *Unsympathisch*—unsympathetic, the man and much of his message. But as long as Thekla can choose what to believe in—his promises of equality and of dismantling the ridiculously complicated class structure—she can teach her boys to advance within that system. *Just for now.* She can wait this out. But some of her boys' families don't have the finesse to make that distinction.

Messages change, but the teaching of knowledge is sacred. Certainly school knowledge, like botany and geography; but also life knowledge, like proper manners and good posture, deep breathing and—above all—how to adapt.

*

Thekla has adapted since she was a child, letting slide past her whatever unsettled her. That's what got you through: you let slide past you, like wind, whatever unsettled you, did not stand in its track where it would topple you. Trains were like that, too, that whoosh going right through you. Tolstoy's Anna Karenina on the end of the platform, the hum and quiver of the approaching train rising through her arches and ankles and thighs and waist and collarbone before she steps forward. Killing herself to stop her anguish. And to punish Vronsky. All this over a man. So pointless, to let lust slide into despair. Still, of the Russian writers, Leo Tolstoy is the one Thekla Jansen admires most.

Better check if Russian writers are still allowed.

If not, she must hide them under the floorboards of the pigeon coop with her other banned books until the government wears itself down. Because it can't last. That's what Thekla tells herself whenever she gets furious at yet another indignity. *It can't last.*

"I know how far to Berlin, Fräulein. My *Opa*—"

"Yes, Wolfgang?"

"My *Opa,* he lives in Berlin, and he says it's five hundred sixty-three kilometers."

"Excellent. Would you like to show us on the map?"

*

The two puckered maps on the wall are the same as when Thekla was a student in this very classroom. Sister Mäuschen, who is in charge of supplies, has refused to replace them with the current maps—false maps, she calls them—that shrank Germany's borders after the Great War.

Back then, when lands were confiscated and citizens turned into foreigners, Sister Mäuschen increased her nightly prayers, and she stormed God with her prayers to restore the borders and reunite the German *Volk*. She knew she'd swayed God when, the day after the Reichstag fire, Hitler pressed Hindenburg into signing two emergency decrees that gave him immediate powers to protect the people and to arrest opponents. Sister Mäuschen appreciated his decisiveness, his courage to dispute Germany's guilt for the Great War, and she was willing to offer up certain freedoms—privacy and speech and press and assembly.

*

Shoulders raised to his ears, Wolfgang sprints to the front where the two maps hang between the chalkboard and the papier-mâché sculpture of the Trojan horse the boys built with Fräulein Siderova. One map is of the world, the other of Germany. But they are the same size—*as if that can be,* Wolfgang puzzles, *one country as big as the whole world?*—and they smell like the chairs in his uncle's barbershop. Except this smell is older, buried in the creases.

Wolfgang is the fastest runner in Fräulein Jansen's class, his body thin and long as if built for sprinting great distances. He can't know that he will return from the next war an amputee, both legs shattered at the Russian front. Can't know that there will be another war. How can he know? How can any of them? After all, today is four and three quarters years before *Kristallnacht,* the Night of Broken Glass, when synagogues and Jewish shops and homes will be torn apart. Today is still five and a half years before the German army will invade Poland one Friday dawn in a preemptive attack from the north, the south, and the west.

*

When Markus Bachmann's parents decided to sell their house on Lindenstrasse—a bad choice; a rash choice—the pharmacist offered them half its worth.

Thekla was appalled that anyone would seek to benefit. "At least hold on till you have a better buyer," she told Markus's parents.

Their friends at the synagogue urged them to last it out.

"You're too quick to worry."

"The political pendulum will stabilize. It always does, after it swings too far to one side."

"Hitler won't get away with this for long."

"Even the Rabbi says not to make big changes right now."

"You don't see us leaving."

"If this gets worse, we'll all speak out."

But Markus's parents warned that those who had the most would also lose the most. Quietly, they accepted the pharmacist's offer and began to sell off their collection of carvings. During their final week in Burgdorf, Thekla went to their house every afternoon on her way from school and tutored Markus so he'd have enough assignments while at sea. She didn't accept payment from his parents, though they tried to insist, but she finally let them give her a small altar panel carved by a student of Tilman Riemenschneider in the sixteenth century.

"We haven't been able to sell it," Markus's parents said when they urged Thekla to take it. "And we can't bring everything with us to America."

"It's premature, leaving the country," she told them again.

*

But within a few weeks after Markus left, Jewish children were no longer allowed in her school. Instead, they were taught all their subjects in the synagogue across the street.

Thekla steps toward the window of her classroom. Steadies herself with one hand. *How much do I know? How much must I try to find out? Once you know, it's tricky to keep the knowing at bay, to press it back into the before-knowing.*

Wolfgang aims the pointer at the Rhein where Burgdorf is just a speck against the embankment, then sweeps the pointer north a bit and way to the east. "Berlin," he announces. As he pivots, he has to laugh because he's looking straight through the frog house on the piano, and beyond the glass and the pebbles and the moss and Icarus are his classmates, as if they, too, were inside the frog house.

But his teacher has her back to him. When she was his age, Jewish children went to the synagogue for religious instruction, while Catholic children and Jewish children who were raised Catholic went to St. Martin's. Afterward, they'd all come back here to school for their other subjects.

"See how far Burgdorf is from Berlin?" Wolfgang asks the teacher. When he turns to his classmates for help, they, too, are studying her.

For her birthday last month, they bought her a green wooden frog and hid it in plain sight, waiting for her to find it. Even the boys in the last row could see it sitting inside Icarus's glass house, but their teacher didn't, not even when she stood next to it while they sang "Happy Birthday." When they giggled and whispered, she asked what was going on. When Bruno said something was wrong with the frog, Andreas giggled more, and Richard said that the frog hadn't moved all morning—not a lie because this was all about the wooden frog. All worried, their teacher leaned over the glass house and laughed aloud. Clapped her hands and laughed. "You boys . . . you and your pranks . . ."

*

The boys' favorite prank is the Trojan horse, the ultimate prank.

But what they want, now, is for their teacher to turn away from the window and toward them, tug at her blue-and-yellow scarf so the blue lies at her collarbone. Sometimes they're sure she wears that scarf just for them. But they've also seen her wear it with her camel hair coat when she walks arm in arm with Herr Hesping. The boys admire him because he's a famous gymnast who has won more trophies than anyone else in Burgdorf, so famous that the owner of the gymnasts' club hired him as the manager.

Still, at school the teacher belongs to them. She tacks their best work to the walls of their classroom: their puppets and their weather charts; their collages of bark rubbings with flecks of bark; and sketches of the trees that bark came from.

"Fräulein Jansen?" they call out to her.

Even the new boy, Heinz, who's scared to talk in class, murmurs, "Fräulein . . . please?"

But her breath is melting the frost-blossoms on the classroom window.

Must I keep asking till I find out what I'm afraid to know? Or can I decide to be satisfied with not knowing beyond what we are told? Because once I know, must I then come forth with that? The risk—

Chapter 4

SUDDENLY THE BOYS are afraid she's about to vanish through that widening circle of frost, vanish like their old teacher, Fräulein Siderova, whom they adored before this young teacher came to them. Beyond the glass, the pigeons are shadowy outlines like souls with sins on them. From their religion lessons with Herr Pastor Schüler, the boys know their bodies are for carrying their souls around and keeping them pure. Pure means without sins. But that can get tricky because of the near occasion of sin: like when your body wants to throw rocks at another boy's body for pinning you down on the sidewalk; or when your body wants to steal candy cigarettes at Weiler's grocery store; or when your body makes you feel nasty.

*

Sins have to do with commandments. Ten commandments. Some are clear enough, like you shall not murder, and you shall not steal.

But some the priest had to explain to the boys, like bearing false witness, which means lying. Most of the boys have lied. But not killed. And not stolen—except that in itself can be a lie, or rather bearing false witness. When the boys asked what it means to covet your neighbor's wife, Herr Pastor Schüler warned that impure thoughts can sneak inside your soul and that you must be vigilant. Because if your soul gets lost, that's it. Hell.

Now, your body is the tool of the Devil. That's why your body gets stinky. Your soul does not smell—except, maybe, of holy water, evidence that you've been to mass. God and Devil fight all day long for souls. And when it's night in Burgdorf, God and Devil fight for the souls of people on the day-side of the world.

*

The boys wonder if Fräulein Jansen is by the window with her back to them because she is disgusted with their sins. Already, they miss her terribly. For her, they are willing to stop their bodies from sinning. That's what their souls are for, they've learned from the priest. And for that, your soul needs the conscience, the tool of God, which is fastened to your soul with ribbons. Red ribbons. Or maybe white ribbons. The priest didn't know for sure when the boys asked him, but he said they were strong ribbons, almost like chains. Whenever your conscience yanks those ribbon-chains, it's to alert your soul that your body is about to stain your soul, maybe for eternity, which means you'll end up living in hell. Or at least in purgatory, where it's not as hot and you have a chance of getting out and ascending to heaven after thirty years, say, or a thousand years. So, whenever you ignore the nagging of your conscience, you should remember that you're weakening it more, tipping the seesaw from right to wrong.

*

When the teacher finally turns toward them, the boys are so relieved that the souls switch back into pigeons, strutting past the space cleared by their teacher's exhalations.

"An anniversary . . . ," she says softly, "will evoke the actual day of it happening, evoke all its sadness or its joy. Can you name some of your own anniversaries?"

"When our baby came out dead," Otto says, though he's learned not to speak of the baby because it makes his mother cry. But he'd say anything to keep his teacher here.

How sad, she thinks. Otto's family must have told him his sister was born dead—not that she died when his mother carried her home from the hospital in a shopping net. Dignity could get in your way of asking for help. Ruin you. People lost their shops and restaurants and offices. Were afraid of starving, of living on the streets. Quite a few killed themselves. So many layers of poverty—depending on how much there was between you and nothing. And how long you could last if you never had food again.

*

One Sunday last December, when Otto was playing at Markus's house, the teacher arrived with schoolbooks for Markus to take with him to America. Twice, she hugged Markus, crying, but she didn't hug Otto. When she gave Markus her own pocket dictionary, *Deutsch-Englisch,* Otto felt slighted. He didn't have anything that had belonged to her.

"Maybe I'll go to America, too," he told her.

But Markus had relatives in America, his Tante Trina, in whose house Markus and his family would live. While Otto didn't have anyone in America. Except—

Except for Markus.

Once the teacher was outside, Otto and Markus watched her from the high bathroom window. They had to stand on the toilet, elbows on the windowsill. On the crusty snow, the soles of their teacher's boots squeaked, and when she got to the big puddle that was frozen hard, she took a run and slid on the ice like a girl. The boys thought she was playing. Until she knelt on the ice and pounded it with her bare fists, mouth open to the sky, screaming.

*

Jochen Weskopp darts into the classroom, rain scattering from his coat, and the floor is all wet again.

"I'm sorry for being late, Fräulein Jansen." Jochen is good with apologies.

Too good, his teacher thinks.

He raises his arm. "Heil Hitler."

"Heil Hitler," she responds.

She used to worry about forgetting to salute and that the students would tell on her, but with each month she's become more immune to her distaste. *They're just words.* At first she avoided raising her arm whenever possible, and she'd move her lips without saying the words aloud. But that became an effort because she'd be monitoring herself to keep from getting caught.

It has become simpler to salute whenever she enters and leaves her classroom. Or when a student, usually Jochen, arrives late.

If I were his mother—

Thekla has spoken to Frau Weskopp, who gets her sons off to school at the same time. While the youngest, Benjamin, is never late, Jochen has to look closely at everything along the way. Still, the other students benefit from his observations because he talks about them in class.

To think I could have children that age.

But Thekla's yearning, all along, has been for students—not for children of her own. Perhaps the yearning, itself, was similar, but she has seen too many mothers sacrificing for their families. Birth children could hold her back. Her students she could bring forward and release. They weren't hers to start out with.

"Please, sit down quietly," she tells Jochen.

But he announces, "My father is getting a new dog for his birthday."

"What kind of dog?" Eckart is poking inside his left ear.

"The same. A *Schäferhund*—sheepdog." Jochen still has his child-face. His brother, too. Some boys keep that child-face into manhood; with others the man-face emerges before they are one year old.

Jochen's father, Konrad, was the first boy Thekla kissed when they were both fifteen. Though she liked the kissing, she avoided Konrad Weskopp after he said that now she'd have to marry him. For him, marriage was the logical outcome of kissing. No wonder the next girl he kissed, Lioba, became his fiancée. A three-year engagement till they were old enough to marry.

Konrad Weskopp still likes to hint at their long-ago courtship. Last month he was at mass in his uniform. Afterward he offered Thekla a cigarette.

"Thank you."

He leaned toward her as he lit it. "My son tells me he wants to marry a girl who smiles like his teacher. I realize why."

As she raised her cigarette, he had to take a step back, and she kept the glowing point between them, distracted him by saying what a remarkable student his Jochen was. So easy to ignore a man's interest by pretending it wasn't there.

*

"Have you ever noticed," Franz says, "that people get the same kind of dog again and again?"

"Yes, like poodles for the Buttgereits," Eckart says.

And now the boys are all talking, interrupting one another.

"Poodles are nervous."

"That's why they yip so much."

"I like cocker spaniels best."

The teacher doesn't remind her boys to wait quietly until she calls on them; she wants them to be silly like this, rambunctious. They've been restless, more so with each day they've come closer to today's anniversary of the fire that changed Germany, the world even. Speculations about communists have been on the radio with a fresh pitch of urgency, fanning fear of this enemy ready to strike and undermine the *Vaterland*.

In the past few months, radios have become so cheap that they're in most households now. Although Thekla has considered buying one—just for the music—she hasn't because she doesn't want those rants to invade her home: rants about cultural Bolshevism, about degenerate intellectuals responsible for the decline of family values, about the healthy instinct of the moral majority reclaiming the traditional family.

"That dog from the pay-library chases birds."

"Not just birds. People, too. He bit Fritz Hansen by the river."

"That dog limps."

"The taxidermist's dog has bad breath and pees inside the house."

Tomorrow she'll bring her boys a poem about courage. A new poem, as every Wednesday. She'll find one that'll uplift them, and if she hasn't already memorized it, she'll copy it into her notebook instead of bringing the thick book of poems collected by Dr. Theodor Echtermeyer generations ago.

The book used to belong to Fräulein Siderova. Until last fall Thekla kept it open on her desk at school so that her students could leaf through the pages, over seven hundred marked pages in a worn binding. Occasionally, she let one of her boys choose the poem for the week and, just like Fräulein Siderova, encouraged her students to mark up pages in the Echtermeyer so that their notes would become part of the text.

*

At home she'll open the book and check the topics in back: courage and sacrifice; happiness and fulfillment; parting and longing; memory and hope. Under "courage" she'll find "*Der Taucher*"—"The Diver" by Friedrich von Schiller. Twenty-seven stanzas. She still recalls every word about the mad king who challenges his knights and pages to dive into the rough sea and retrieve the golden cup he's tossing from the cliff. Glory, he promises. Wealth. Only one young page, *sanft und keck*—mild and audacious, leaps in despite the danger and vanishes down the chasm. But he emerges with the cup, with tales of the horrors below the surface, and he warns the others not to tempt the gods by longing to see what they, mercifully, cover with night and horror.

Da unten aber ist's fürchterlich,
Und der Mensch versuche die Götter nicht
Und begehre nimmer und nimmer zu schauen,
Was sie gnädig bedecken mit Nacht und Grauen.

Tomorrow she'll recite "*Der Taucher*" to her boys, the way Fräulein Siderova used to teach poems. Every Wednesday, Fräulein Siderova would recite a new poem and write it on the chalkboard. Thursdays her students would copy it from the chalkboard. Fridays she'd divide her class into four groups so that each group, *en chorus,* could chant one stanza. And by Saturday every one of Fräulein Siderova's students would be able to recite the entire poem.

Thekla still remembers how terrified she felt for the diver when the king, once more, flung the cup into the roiling sea and promised him marriage to his daughter if he leapt in again and brought him more knowledge of what lay beneath. Even as a girl Thekla understood what hubris it was to ask that much of fate. But he leapt, the young page.

Of course he was flung against the cliffs.

Of course he drowned.

*

Legends and poetry were filled with stories of hubris that lured you into death, and Thekla's students were mesmerized by those stories. That's why they voted to change their frog's name from Copernicus to Icarus the morning she taught them about Icarus's flight toward the sun.

To escape from King Minos, Icarus's father, Daedalus, built wings for his son and himself. After they practiced leaping into the air with those wings—"like frogs," the boys pointed out—Daedalus and Icarus soared away. But Icarus became cocky, ignored his father's warnings, and flew toward the sun. Of course, its heat melted the wax between his feathers and sent him tumbling back to earth.

When Andreas Beil concluded that Icarus died because he was disobedient to his father, the teacher was not about to reduce legend to a moral about obedience, and she asked her boys to sketch the wings of Icarus. It was well known that Andreas's father was too strict. Children who were confined, body or mind, often strained against that confinement, and she could certainly see that in Andreas, who bullied other children. Yet, he was also gifted at sketching, and that's what she focused on when she praised him for his intricate picture of wooden frames with feathers held together by wax.

*

Thekla has inherited this class of seventeen boys from Fräulein Siderova. There were five more when she started last May, but she's lost them: David, Hans, Jakob, and Simon attend school at the synagogue; and Markus is in America. She feels accountable to Fräulein Siderova, who has lodged herself within her like conscience itself.

You know what it's like, Fräulein Siderova, studying for the work you're meant to do. But you have no idea what it's like to wait for ten years. You found a teaching position right away.

Sometimes Thekla wants her out of her head, just for a while, but then she'll open her drawer in the teachers' lounge where Fräulein Siderova used to keep her books and handbag, and she's overcome by the familiar scent of rosewater and vanilla, by the urgency to help her teacher.

Soon, I'll invite you to visit my class. Except, I don't want Sister Josefine to say something that would . . . offend you. Better to invite you along on a learning excursion. In the spring. No need to tell anyone at school. I'll let you know where I'll be with the boys, and you'll meet us . . . as if by chance, yes, or maybe watch us from a distance.

On Thekla's bedroom wall with the family photos hangs one of Fräulein Siderova tending her indoor garden in her tall bay window, where stained glass will coax light even from hazy days.

*

Every Sunday afternoon when Thekla visits Fräulein Siderova, she's dazzled by the light coming through the stained glass, diffusing and reassembling itself around her so that she feels part of the light, light herself, in a shape that is only hers.

For decades, the people of Burgdorf have thought of Fräulein Siderova as a midwife to the dying, and they've sent for her to read poetry to their dying in her lovely voice, guiding them right up to that threshold of death, but letting them cross it alone while she stayed behind. She knew how to. Knew enough about everyone to choose poems that were meaningful for that person alone—poems about courtship or nature or victory—that led the dying back to those people who had once inhabited, or still inhabited, their sorrow: an unforgiving parent, say, or a false love, or, worst of all, an already dead child; and as the dying encountered them on this final passage, they felt ready to let them be. As they were and would be.

Fräulein Siderova wouldn't accept money for this, but since it was known that she adored stained glass, the townspeople would give her the most precious of what they'd inherited or what they could buy for her: a translucent blue vase, say, or a Venetian goblet, or a bowl so yellow it held the sun in its center.

*

Every Sunday afternoon when Thekla visits, Fräulein Siderova gets out her Russian porcelain cups and brews red tea from rosehips that she gathers every August and dries—

—except that's no longer true—

*

Every Sunday afternoon when Thekla visits—

—except I haven't visited you, Fräulein Siderova, though I've thought every day about coming to you—

Her heartbeat against her clavicle, Thekla longs for her teacher's praise, the joy of it.

I haven't dared visit you in nine months—

1899

Chapter 5

LOVE COULD BE TRICKY, the nuns at the St. Margaret Home knew. It could make you crazy for one night, or forever. Make you lie to yourself and deceive others. Make you long for secret touches you ought to forget but tried to remember. And because the nuns understood this, they tried to protect the St. Margaret Girls, made them wear gray capes to hide their shame. Yet, those capes only identified them.

Named after the patron saint of childbirth, the St. Margaret Home was the largest industry on the Nordstrand peninsula, the industry of illegitimacy, that provided income for the convent and gave the nuns purposeful work: tending to the souls and bodies of pregnant young women, the youngest barely fifteen years old, the oldest past thirty, who arrived here frightened but relieved to be far enough from home so people wouldn't talk.

The Nordstrand peninsula was shielded by islands that buffered the coast from the moods and the direct onrush of the Nordsee—

North Sea. Over the centuries, children had played on the tidal flats; couples had strolled at sunset; and horses had pulled the people of Nordstrand in carriages and sleds. Here, by the edge of the Nordsee, earth and water had barely separated and were still as they must have been on the third day of creation. That's what the children of Nordstrand learned in school and in church, how God had separated land from water, scooped his hands into the masses of water, sifted the muck by holding it raised till all water had drained away, and named the residue: land.

But the midwife, Lotte Jansen, knew there was no God. Of course, she kept this secret from the nuns who employed her to bring life into the world. At the St. Margaret Home, she was known for her kindness and skillful hands, but most of all because not one single death happened on her watch. It was said that her great tragedy protected anyone she touched because death would be embarrassed to come near her again.

*

In the dining room of the Home hung a diptych of St. Margaret. In the first panel, the patron saint of pregnant women was swallowed by a dragon. Actually, it was the devil disguised as a dragon. But—by divine preordination, so it was said—St. Margaret clutched her book-size cross as she was being sucked down the tunnel of the dragon's throat. The edges of her cross scraped and pierced the lining of the dragon's throat, causing his engorged body to contract, a brutal reminder—the midwife thought—to the pregnant Girls of what they had yet to endure. That's why she advised them to sit with their backs to the picture while they ate.

When the train with Almut Bechtel arrived on Nordstrand in the spring of 1899, it slowed before it reached the station, crossing vast meadows with sheep and cattle and horses. One mare stood in the backyard of a small farm, nuzzling a foal that lay on its side, all four legs stretched in one direction, as if felled from the effort of being born. *I don't have to think of that yet,* Almut told herself. *I don't have to think about that till the day it wants to be born, and then I can be as afraid as I need to be. I know I can get through what needs to be gotten through.*

She'd been on trains all day, leaving Burgdorf before dawn. At the St. Margaret Home, a kind nun with wide hands gave her a gray woolen cape and words of caution about the steep marble stairs between the second floor and the third-floor dormitories, where one might take a shallow step and fall and lose one's baby.

*

When Almut entered the dining room, she came to a halt in front of the diptych, studied the first panel without flinching, and laughed aloud at the second panel, where St. Margaret stood above the felled dragon, one bare foot on his green lizard skin, her raised cross dripping with dragon gore, her dress immaculate.

"Why would you be laughing?" the midwife asked.

"I can get out the worst stains . . . coal and blood and gravy and red wine. But that dress?"

"No?"

"How can it be that white after her ordeal?"

"Proof of her virginity?"

"Please!"

The midwife's face opened into one of the rare smiles that let others forget her sorrow, and she motioned the new St. Margaret Girl to sit with her. *Here's one who won't be broken either.*

While Almut ate her lentil soup, she considered the panel. "That picture is a lie," she concluded. "Because I could not get that dress clean again."

"Are you practical? Or irreverent?"

"Both," Almut said without hesitation.

It started there for the two women, the recognition of something kindred; and from that day forward, a friendship grew as they sat next to each other at meals, facing the diptych to mock it and to spare others the sight.

*

Between the St. Margaret Home and the St. Margaret Church, an alley of birches and more substantial chestnut trees arched above the brick path, concealing the St. Margaret Girls on their walk to mass. To keep the Girls from distracting the parishioners, the Girls had to use the side door. They were the first to enter, the last to leave, causing the younger children of the parish to assume the St. Margaret Girls lived and slept in these pews.

As Almut Bechtel followed the pregnant Girls into the pews to the left, beneath the pulpit, the smell of the ancient stone floor and painted stone walls reminded her of her cellar in Burgdorf. One of the altar boys latched the low gate at the end of each pew before the parishioners began to arrive through the large main doorway, pouring down the center aisle, where they genuflected and separated, filing into long pews on the women's or the men's side of the church.

When the old priest lumbered up the steps to the black and gold pulpit, his sermon fell on the St. Margaret Girls as though it were the voice of God.

They all worked in the nursery of the Home, longing for the day when their bellies would be flat again, their infants adopted by kind families, and they could return to their hometowns with stories to be believed, stories they revised during pregnancy as they inspired one another, a story of visiting an ailing godmother in Bremen, say, or sitting by the deathbed of a grandfather who'd made death wait for seven months.

*

While the nuns counseled the St. Margaret Girls on abstinence, the midwife counseled them on pregnancy and birth. Some were so naïve that she had to explain how they'd come to be with child. They'd been seduced, or forced, or had yielded to the confusing insistence of their own bodies. What the midwife's patients had in common was that they felt trapped and wanted to be separate, once again, from what was crowding them inside. Some had tried old-fashioned methods of prevention: jumping backward seven times after intercourse to dislodge the seeds, or rotating their hips during intercourse to keep the seeds from attaching, or catching a frog and spitting into the frog's mouth three times, or tying a pouch with a cat's liver around one ankle.

The midwife shuddered to imagine what had happened to the rest of the cat. She was impatient with myths that lured women into trusting they wouldn't get pregnant. That's why, secretly, she helped those St. Margaret Girls who asked her how to avoid pregnancies. Since nearly all would leave without their babies, they didn't have the choice that married women had: to breast-feed for a year or more, as the midwife had with her own babies, thereby tricking their bodies into presuming they were already pregnant. But what the midwife could do was insert a little wooden block in front of the cervix before her patient reentered the outside world. These blocks the midwife ordered from local toymakers by the dozen—smooth and unpainted with rounded edges—allowing the men who sanded them to assume they were for the children at the St. Margaret Home. To let them find out that these blocks served to prevent children would have meant banishment.

The making of toys was the second largest industry on the peninsula; but since there were too many toymakers—as if to make up for too many babies—the apprentices would donate their experiments to the St. Margaret Home, where the children who'd been left behind got to play with toys that were unlike others and would never reach the market.

Some toymakers felt sorry for these children when Lotte Jansen ordered her plain blocks, and they couldn't stop themselves from carving pictures into the surfaces of these blocks and painting them with their brightest colors, feeling generous as they imagined the joy of the children.

Of course, Lotte would thank them and hand the blocks to the children who did, indeed, enjoy them. Then she'd order another dozen—smooth and unpainted with rounded edges—from a different toy shop until, finally, she found one that did not improve her order.

*

There were always St. Margaret Girls who felt guilty about releasing their children for adoption. They knew the midwife would not judge them because what she'd done to her youngest was a thousand times worse than giving your child away to a decent family. That's why they trusted her, came to her with their guilt. Some did sign the papers, then; but others wanted to wait with deciding, leave their infants in limbo at St. Margaret's, where a new crop of pregnant Girls would feed them and bathe them and murmur endearments their own children would never hear from them.

Here, in spacious rooms lined with cribs and tall windows, these children learned to walk and pray and sing. A few of their mothers would visit with gifts and with tears. Most would not return. Still, you'd come to recognize them in towns afar or near because they'd glance away from children as if stung, or they'd stare at them with such hunger that children would want to hide from them.

Once or twice a year, a new mother would insist on taking her child with her, raise it alone. Foolish, the nuns would say. Yet, they'd bundle diapers and clothes and tiny blankets for her to take along, advise her to tell people she was a new widow. It would bring her compassion. Respect.

*

For twenty-one years, Lotte Jansen had known there was no God.

She had still believed in God that August day she'd taken her four children to the traveling Zirkus. On the way home, they'd run onto the tidal flats as they often did, laughing and chasing after the tide that would retreat for kilometers, Lotte with the baby, Wilhelm, in one arm, her other children linked to her by holding hands: Bärbel with her tiny fingers clenched around Lotte's thumb; Martin in the middle; her oldest, Hannelore, on the outside.

Clouds of seagulls rose from the damp flats, an entire sky in each vale between the sand ridges that would fill once again in a few hours when the incoming tide would meld a thousand skies into one. But for now it was only sand that squeezed itself up between their toes, golden and wet, sand and shallow puddles that sloshed around their feet.

Running and laughing with her children, Lotte, because tomorrow she would take them to the Zirkus again, for free again, because their father, like other toymakers on Nordstrand, worked there as a roustabout for a week every summer. Running and singing with her children, Lotte, *wunschlos glücklich*—happy without a wish, until another sound muffled the screeching of the seagulls and the laughter of her children, a roaring, a rushing, as a freak wave galloped at them—

No—

Too soon for the tide to—

She had never seen a wave that colossal. "Hold on to each other!" Lotte shouted and tightened her grip on Bärbel. "Deep breath! Duck into the wave—" Because that was how she and her husband, Kalle, had taught their three oldest to swim. That's how all the people on Nordstrand learned to swim as small children, facing a wave and then ducking into it before it curled, before it could tumble them.

But Lotte had never been seized by a wave this crushing. Still, she believed in God when it toppled and spun and choked her, when she burst into light, dizzy and coughing, with her youngest in her arm—

Both arms—

"Bärbel—" she screamed. "Martin—Hannelore—"

They were bobbing just two church-lengths away from her as the wave took them toward the horizon, then four church-lengths, leaving behind nothing but soaked ground. Clutching Wilhelm, Lotte ran after them to where she'd spotted them last—*Bärbel Martin Hannelore*—pushing at God with her prayers, her rage.

She still believed in God while the townspeople and the Zirkus people fanned across the tidal flats, clowns and acrobats still in their costumes, side by side with farmers and nuns and toymakers. Most hunted the wave on foot, but some rode out on horses and Zirkus ponies.

Even when Kalle reminded her what good little swimmers their children were, Lotte still believed in God. Even when the tide came back in and divers searched for the children, Lotte believed God was keeping them afloat nearby until the sea would spit them out.

And it was the immensity of her belief in this all-powerful and all-merciful God that led to her bargain with God. She drew the sign of the cross on her baby's heart, kissed his lips, his forehead. "Take Wilhelm in return for the other three," she wailed and flung him into the sea.

But God did not keep Wilhelm. And that's how she knew there was no God. Kalle scrambled into the sea, horrified by what his wife had done, and raised his youngest into his arms. At home, he laid the boy against Lotte's breast, and she cupped Wilhelm's head in her palm the way she had with all her children. But her breasts had gone bone-dry, and Wilhelm twisted his face aside.

When Kalle sent to the priest for help, he arrived with Sister Franziska and a St. Margaret Girl who'd recently given birth. From her, Wilhelm accepted the breast, so hungry that he was sobbing with each swallow.

For five days, Kalle tried to look into his Lotte's face, to match his sorrow to hers. But he couldn't. When he left with the Zirkus, the people of Nordstrand said he could have forgiven his wife for losing three of his children to the sea—a wave like that happened once in a lifetime, no, once in a hundred years—but that he would never forgive her for what she'd done to Wilhelm.

*

The nuns understood Lotte Jansen's sorrow. Scripture and life had taught them about sacrifice, about a mother offering up her child to God. They brought Lotte and Wilhelm to the St. Margaret Home. While she slept or cried in the small room next to the dormitory, Wilhelm lived in the nursery where Sister Franziska, the midwife, would rock him, play with him, and tell him stories of the Virgin Maria who had relinquished her son to God when he was thirty-three.

During the weeks and months his mother was lost to Wilhelm, he was breast-fed by St. Margaret Girls who'd given up their infants soon after birth and pitied this boy who brought them relief from the fullness in their breasts. But some were so shocked by an unforeseen longing for their own babies that they wouldn't go near Wilhelm again.

When Lotte was able to sit up in her bed, she could see across the dike and the edges of land that had been reclaimed so often from the Nordsee that the people were accustomed to shifting ground beneath their feet and beneath their houses, even in their connections to others because those, too, could be washed away. In a landscape like this, you could not presume.

*

Twice a day, Sister Franziska would carry Wilhelm up the marble steps to the third floor, lay him on the pillow next to his mother's face, and quietly sing to them both. Once Lotte was ready to get up, Sister Franziska offered her paying work, trained her in the nursery, then in the delivery room, though Lotte was terrified that her touch might cause death.

Sister Franziska would listen, nod, then fill the young woman's arms with newborns. For each of her own, lost, Lotte helped another child into the world. Then ten. Thirty. And more until she, too, had become a midwife.

Every dawn, Lotte Jansen would walk by herself along the edge of the sea. Some people said it was odd; others speculated she was still waiting for her drowned children. But there were enough people, including the priest, who believed the legend of Rungholt, a wealthy city swallowed by the Nordsee over five centuries ago; they found it comforting to think of Lotte imagining her children safe in Rungholt, surrounded by treasures and toys made of gold.

Wilhelm grew accustomed to nights at home with his mother and days with other children in the nursery of the St. Margaret Home, where his mother was the one who fed him, rocked him, and came back to play with him whenever she could between patients. His mother and Sister Franziska fussed over him because he had trouble filling his skin and drew unsettling pictures of a boy with dark waves inside his head.

He would not forget the briny taste of the sea, and he'd become a slight man with pale eyes and pale hair, a boy of a man who'd never quite reclaim his flesh from the water-grave of his siblings. He'd become a toymaker like his father, who continued to work for the Zirkus, where he used his skills to repair broken equipment, wheels and poles and yokes, and carve toy animals, tigers and elephants and monkeys and giraffes, that he sold outside the tent whenever the Zirkus arrived in a new place.

Chapter 6

It was at Sunday mass where Wilhelm Jansen first saw Almut Bechtel, enfolded in the honey-colored light from the stained-glass windows, where she knelt in the St. Margaret Home pews with other Girls in gray capes. Her freckles and her hair were the color of honey, too, so that she seemed to be made of light and of joy, and the toymaker believed that she was the opposite of him and that he could love her.

That's what he heard himself say aloud when he waited for her after mass—"I believe I could love you"—when what he'd intended to say was that he'd like to invite her on a walk.

Of course she shook her head.

Of course he was mortified.

Of course he was certain, in the week that followed, that he could never again enter this church where he'd been christened and had received first communion. If necessary, he would become a Protestant to avoid her.

*

Yet, the following Sunday the young toymaker was back—to apologize to her, he believed—and knelt in the last pew on the men's side of the church. Quite a few of the men were watching the St. Margaret Girls, speculating that it was easier to sweet-talk women into opening their legs once they'd done it, because doing it made them need it from then on. Even the toymaker, still a virgin, found himself thinking that, and he felt so ashamed that he fled while the priest gave the final blessing.

He made it to the bottom of the church steps before a voice called out to him. "Wait . . ."

Feeling caught and prickly, he turned.

The St. Margaret Girl with the freckles stood on the top step, her boots at the same level as his eyes—sturdy and laced to above her ankles, old leather made smooth with much polish and brushing—and he thought how odd her boots looked with her church dress, which hung in pleats from her shoulders beneath her open cape.

He hoped she didn't think he was pretty. He'd heard people say that about his father, that he was too pretty.

Almut was thinking how beautiful he was, this man with the fine-boned features. Pointing her toes inward, she motioned to them and grimaced. "I wore my hiking boots to mass. . . . In case you'd still like to take a walk?"

He laughed with relief, no longer certain what he had said to her. His words and thoughts must have become jumbled so that, indeed, he had invited her for a walk.

"Yes," he said. "Yes."

*

He walked with her along the top of a dike where sheep grazed on both slopes, one curving down toward the ocean, the other toward the windmills and the brick or stucco houses. Some of the older sheep were so huge that, when they lay down, their backs spread as wide as a child's mattress. But the lambs were running and hopping, kicking their hind legs.

"Like fawns," Almut said with delight.

Fields of rapeseed stretched beyond the neighborhoods, yellow and swaying.

"*Raps,*" Wilhelm said. "People make oil from it. Honey, too."

"Your clouds are different from where I come from," she said.

"In what way?"

She pointed toward one of the islands where wind bunched the clouds into tight formations. "The way they move. With a river, they move in streaks, like the current, almost." She spoke in a dialect that enchanted him because it was like singsong running alongside words.

He told her about his fear of the sea, about the gray waves inside his head that claimed him time and again; and as she listened, closely, he could see she wasn't afraid of him.

"Maybe," she said, "it's because you have the fanciful mind that goes with making toys . . . with dreaming."

"This is not like dreaming." He told her about his sisters and brother drowning, about his mother pulling him from the sea and then flinging him back in, about a pale sky suddenly tilted and replaced by muddy water.

Almut reached for his hand. "I've heard."

"I think I know why. Because—how could she not?"

"I don't know what to say."

"Wouldn't you trade one child for three?"

"I won't even keep this one."

"Don't you wish you could keep it?"

"It wouldn't be . . . practical."

He took that in. Waited.

"I already promised to let it be adopted."

Damp air shimmered around them, silver-gray air the color of sky, of water, shimmering and holding them separate from the rest of Nordstrand, and he realized he was afraid of losing her. And her child. How could that be? He barely knew her.

He moved his shoulder so she could lean against it, and when she did, he asked her, "What if you could raise the child . . . you and a husband?"

*

When he asked his mother if he could invite Almut Bechtel to their house for coffee and cake, she said yes and of course.

The following Sunday, after he left to pick Almut up at the St. Margaret Home, his mother set the table in the living room with her best china and tablecloth. She cooked coffee and whipped cream to serve with the *Erdbeertorte*—strawberry tart she'd baked that morning. Behind the lace curtain, she waited for them, heart beating—*for what?*—for what she didn't let herself hope.

When her son led Almut into the house, the midwife stepped forward and took both her hands. "I am so glad," she said. And then said it again. "I am so glad."

Wilhelm seemed boylike next to Almut, though he was older—just by a month; still, older—and for an instant the midwife was afraid he might not be enough for Almut. And yet, there was something different about Wilhelm, passion, and it felt odd to notice that about her quiet son, unfamiliar and surprising. Suddenly, the midwife felt taller without the familiar weight of her worry for him.

Chapter 7

EVERY SATURDAY AFTERNOON the toymaker went to confession, knelt on the outside of the wooden latticework, and received absolution and penance: twelve Hail Marys plus six Our Fathers for lusting after a pregnant woman.

That August, when Almut had been on Nordstrand five months, the old priest informed her during her confession that the toymaker was eager to save her from shame.

Her face burned. "Is that what he told you?"

"Your initial sin has been confessed properly and—"

Your initial sin, succumbing to being needed that morning in the kitchen when Michel Abramowitz touches your elbow, courteous and kind and something unfamiliar, too, his urgency that makes you feel chosen, and you know he'll stop if you say so, that's why you don't need to stop him, still, as he raises you, there's an instant of doubt, yet to push him away now would make you a . . . a bad hostess, no, not hostess, there has to be a better word, and whatever it is, you're not like that word, but just then you're stunned by your own moaning need that cleaves you in half and—

Your initial sin. Your one-time-only sin. Both of you horrified. Afterward. Even before afterward begins.

"—and absolved properly," the priest continued, "but you must know—"

"To save me from shame? Is that what Wilhelm Jansen said." Her words bounced off the priest's body. They had nowhere to go because his bulk and smell filled the cubicle of the dim confessional. Back home, with skinny Pastor Schüler, there'd always been enough air between him and Almut.

She shifted to ease the pressure of wood against her knees. Again, she asked him, "Is that what Wilhelm Jansen said?"

"Not like that, no, Fräulein Bechtel."

He called me by my name? She had believed you could tell a priest everything because you were anonymous in the confessional. Bound by his vows, a priest would rather endure torture or death than reveal your name and sins to others. How about all those stories of murderers confessing, unburdening themselves, knowing the priests could never turn them over to the police?

"You called me by my name," Almut told the priest. "That's wrong."

"You must know that to continue sinning like this will mean losing your soul and residing in hell forever. It is God's will that you marry the toymaker."

"Not like this."

"The toymaker is a shy man. He doesn't think you'd want to be his wife. But it's God's will."

There was not enough air between her and this priest's wall of flesh.

"Think of your soul," he pressed.

Priests, Almut thought, were the same no matter where. That pious and lust-denying façade of theirs squeezed women into chastity and corsets. And yet, she still needed the solace of church. Still. Already, she had confessed far too much to this priest.

"Think of your child's soul," he warned.

Your child's soul. That, too. Soul and bones and skin . . . and how you imagine Michel leaving his wife when you tell him you're with child . . . and how instead he confesses to his wife—

No more confessing—

Dizzy in the moist August heat, Almut Bechtel raised herself from her knees.

"Wait—" the priest called after her, one hand flailing from the confessional in a lopsided blessing. "Remember . . . in the face of God, my dear child."

*

The following Saturday, in the very same confessional, the toymaker was assigned his usual twelve Hail Marys and six Our Fathers for lusting after a pregnant woman. He crossed himself and left the confessional. In a pew, nearby, knelt that very same pregnant woman as though he'd summoned her with his sin, and she beckoned him to her. When he knelt by her side, she opened one button of her gray cape, pulled his hand inside where her belly was taut, high, where it felt holier than church with his hand against her belly beneath her cape, and he wanted to stay like this in the amber light with her and the child who was part of her.

"Still?" She raised her face to him.

"Still," he said because he knew what she was about to ask him.

And she did. "You still believe you could love me?"

"Even more so."

She closed her eyes, and her face grew composed, as if—Wilhelm thought—she was allowing herself to love her child. Until this moment, she must have steeled herself to let another family raise it; but now her palm slid across the back of his hand that lay on her belly, and as he felt enveloped by the child and by her, he wanted to say, "Who could possibly be a better father than a maker of toys?" But it felt too light, felt only half true, felt as though he suspected her of wanting to marry him for his name only. Just then she opened her eyes to him, and he was struck by the force of her love, on him now, too.

*

That Sunday he took her in the horse-drawn carriage up the school hill, the highest point on the peninsula, and told her it was the custom on Nordstrand to propose on the tidal flats at sunset.

She smiled. "So that's why you and I are not on the tidal flats?"

"No," he said. "I mean, yes. Because I can't . . ."

"Go out there again. I know."

"But will you?"

"Yes."

"I mean— Will you? Marry me?"

"Yes."

"Really?"

"Really."

"Why?"

"Because—"

"I can't believe I asked why."

"Because of your kindness. Because of your beauty—"

He groaned. "I'm not beautiful."

"Because I like your face. Because I can't stop thinking of you at night."

Wilhelm blushed. She had told him he was inventive, joyful, and he was trying to be all that for her.

"Because you are brave."

Brave? He shook his head. "Being brave is not in me."

"It is brave to marry a woman who carries another man's child."

He winced.

"Do you want me to tell you who he is?"

Up here all around them the land was dry, but the slopes were increasingly damp where they descended into soggy marshes, where wind swept through tall grasses with such recklessness that they heaved like waves.

"Don't," he said, quickly, because if he let her, she would tell him the other man's name. In all truth.

She studied him.

"I don't want you to be lost to me," he said.

From the village, people could see the back of the carriage but not inside, where Almut unbuttoned Wilhelm's shirt. At first he was anxious about the child whose movements rippled the wall of Almut's belly, but when she let him know with her body how she wanted him, straddled him, he stunned himself, and her. This here— This— He was good at this, amazingly so . . . this giving of pleasure and this taking of pleasure all at once or not all at once, and already he knew this would be there from now on—for him, and between him and Almut—his to return to even if the shadow wings were to spread again.

*

Wilhelm adored the girl who was born one month and four days after his wedding to Almut. Long-limbed and narrow, with beautiful hands, Thekla smiled like a child who'd never been at risk of not having a father, and he took that as trust in him and devoted himself to her. For weeks at a time, he'd forget that she hadn't come from his seed. She was here, and she was his.

From *Kirschholz*—cherrywood he carved a kitten that slept curled in one smooth ball, too wide for this daughter to fit into her mouth, too light if she were to drop it on her belly. He sanded the reddish golden wood till it felt silky. His mother showed him how to comfort his daughter when she was crying, and he'd lay Thekla on his knees, her back on his thighs, and bounce her gently, one hand rubbing her belly.

*

Though Wilhelm found an apartment as far as possible from the St. Margaret Home, some gossiped that of course the child did not resemble him with her bold gaze and brown curls, that his love for her sapped him of the honor he'd offered her mother in marriage.

But Lotte Jansen sensed that Almut had chosen her son because he needed her strength as much as she needed his name. Almut would never have just taken the respect that came with his name for her child and herself—she wasn't like that—but she was giving Wilhelm confidence, joy.

It enraged the midwife when people whispered, "The toymaker has a *Kuckuck*—cuckoo in his nest." *Kuckucks* were lazy, and because they didn't like to sit on their eggs, they laid them in the nests of other birds, tricking those birds into raising them.

She'd been the center of gossip for so much of her life that she'd taught herself it was none of her concern what others said about her. But this was different: this gossip was hurting her son and his new family. That's why Lotte Jansen turned on anyone who—under the guise of compassion—urged her to confide. "My daughter-in-law is hardworking and kind," she'd say. "It is an honor to have her in my family."

On Nordstrand, gossip would always be part of her daughter-in-law's life. Here, marriage led not to acceptance but to the loss of pity. Over the last quarter century, nineteen pregnant St. Margaret Girls had snagged—so it was said—local fellows into marriage and instant fatherhood, depriving local girls of potential husbands. But despite marriage, the status of St. Margaret brides remained below that of brides who'd waited till they were properly wed before spreading their legs, and birthed only children who were legitimately conceived.

That stigma of illegitimate birth haunted the St. Margaret mothers and their children, their grandchildren even, so that in a store or church someone might say, "*Ach ja,* your grandmother was a St. Margaret Girl."

Tuesday, February 27, 1934

Chapter 8

WE PLANT *STIEFMÜTTERCHEN*—pansies on my *Oma*'s grave every anniversary of her death," says Walter. Crooked teeth but the part in his hair always straight.

"The anniversary of when my cat died," says Wolfgang.

"Please." Fräulein Jansen raises both hands. "Can we please talk about anniversaries of celebrations?"

"My sister's wedding," Andreas Beil offers and flattens the cowlick that juts out above his left ear. Like a tusk, his sister teases him, calls him *Rhinozeros*.

"The anniversary of when my aunt became a nun," says Franz.

"My aunt is a nun, too," says Walter, who likes to draw pictures of Jesus.

"My aunt eats lunch with us every Sunday," says Franz.

"But my aunt stayed with us when my *Oma* was sick," says Walter.

"My uncle is a priest in Oberkassel," Jochen says.

As Thekla steps toward the boys, away from the chill of the window, she can see how exhilarated they are to pull her closer with their words, with the proof of their devotion. *All boys are men. And all men are boys. If you treat them all like ten-year-olds, you'll get their adoration, but you don't have to acknowledge their power. Because for that power to display itself, it needs your acknowledgment of it, too.*

*

But Bruno looks away from her, the skin below his eyes smudged from lack of sleep. She must speak to his parents tonight, make them understand how the uniform would help him to be accepted by his classmates. It does, whenever he smuggles it to school and wears it in the classroom. But that has become complicated now that his mother picks him up for lunch and walks him back to school.

Just last week in the school yard, his first day of no longer wearing his uniform, several boys surrounded him, shoving, yelling.

"Your father will live in hell!"

"Not so!" Bruno cried.

"For all eternity!"

"Protestants don't get to live in heaven!"

"Not so!"

His parents will want to listen to Thekla because it has been a concern before, boys heckling Bruno that his father will go to hell. Herr Stosick is the principal of the Protestant school, but Bruno has to go to Catholic school because his mother would have been excommunicated for marrying a Protestant if they hadn't both promised the priest—long before there was a wedding and a Bruno—to raise all future children as Catholics. Except there was only the one, Bruno, after three stillbirths.

*

"I see a bonding among boys who wear the uniform," Thekla will say to his parents, "stronger than resentments or class differences."

"All that pride and power?" Günther Stosick may ask.

"And what's wrong with pride?" she'll ask him right back. "Haven't we done for long enough without it?"

"We were more human without it." He'll fold his hands in front of his belly. He's not flabby but thickset and strong, with a belly that starts high.

Thekla cannot fathom how Gisela can be attracted to his body. To his mind, yes, he's brilliant; and to his eyes, a gorgeous deep brown. But that belly . . .

"It's about respect for our children," she'll tell both Stosicks. "About a future for our children. The Hitler-Jugend offers them adventure. Equality. It's impossible for a schoolchild to avoid all involvement in youth activities. What harm can it do, letting Bruno go to some meetings? We had songs and bonfires, too."

She just hopes that ugly dog of theirs will be asleep. If not, Henrietta will jam herself against Thekla's thighs again, nudge her to stroke that thick neck, that mottled black fur so short it feels like skin. With the Stosicks right there, Thekla will pet Henrietta. But whenever she's alone with the dog, Thekla keeps some piece of furniture between herself and Henrietta.

"The uniform made such a difference for Richard," she'll tell the Stosicks. "Until then, the boys were merciless with him."

No. That would be inviting the Stosicks to tell her Richard's situation is hardly comparable because he's illegitimate. They may get offended because his mother is one of those widows. Every town has them. Women whose husbands died in the Great War and who resorted to prostitution.

Thekla must be diplomatic with the Stosicks, or she'll lose her apartment. She was lucky to find a place she can afford without needing the Führer's help. Not that his help is available to her. Still, he should grant unmarried teachers the same loan he grants to newlyweds, one thousand marks, almost a year's income. He rewards only married couples. For the birth of each child, he reduces the loan by a quarter, motivating women to push one child after another from their bodies. After four children for the *Vaterland,* the families owe nothing. So unjust to the teachers who devote themselves to the children of those families.

*

Ever since Thekla was three, she has known she was a teacher. Knowing began the afternoon she found a chestnut by the flour mill and gave it to her father, Wilhelm, who was ill again, sitting by the stove in his black suit, eyes pale and winter-still, hands like fallen twigs on his knees. He didn't look at her. Only at the tiny blond hairs between his knuckles. She lifted his left hand, turned it palm up. It was warm. Because that side of him was near the stove. *Mutti* said it was the side where his heart pumped.

Thekla set the chestnut into *Vati*'s palm, took hold of his thumb, and rubbed it across the glossy-brown shell. When his fingers began to quiver, she felt the teaching that lived inside her: *This is what I am, what I want to do.*

His eyes flickered, let her in just long enough to follow him down a shaft toward a blink of lucidity—*so that is where Vati lives when he goes away like this*—follow him deeper yet, down, down so fast it was like falling, and suddenly mist and glitter and color bursting open in his memory—*because of the chestnut and the skin*—and as she felt him reaching for that mist and glitter and color, she became Wilhelm, *was Wilhelm climbing a tree and tossing green apples to his friends . . . was Wilhelm sledding down a hill with a dog chasing him . . . was Wilhelm falling, an infant, Wilhelm*— But already the passage was slamming shut—*because I don't love you enough?*—and he was lost to her. But not forever. Because now Thekla understood it was touch that opened him up—*chestnut and skin brought together by the teacher. By the teacher's way of teaching. Mine*—and that once she knew how to bring him back so he'd be like other fathers, she could love him, too, the way she loved *Mutti.*

Chapter 9

OTTO'S PULSE is in his throat, fast like some nights when he has the teacher under the blanket with him, her hand with his hand there, nasty and beneath the warmth and—

"Did you want to say something, Otto?" his teacher is asking.

He covers his throat to hide his pulse but feels it in his palm, his wrist, nasty, and confession isn't till Saturday.

"Otto?"

What if she can tell by looking at him what he does with her at night?

His belly feels warm, heavy. His belly and his legs. Sins get heavier with each hour you can't confess them.

She nods at him. Waits.

"The anniversary of . . . of my own birthday?"

"Another good example," she praises him. She likes this thoughtful boy who is drawn to the passion of learning. A few of her boys are all brain. While others are all body: Andreas, Wolfgang. But Otto is both.

"You are both," Fräulein Siderova told Thekla when she was a student in this very classroom. "Brain and body. I was so much like you when I was a girl."

"I want to be a teacher, too," Thekla said.

"You will be an amazing teacher," her teacher encouraged her. "A natural and inventive teacher."

*

Fräulein Siderova always had one favorite student—allowed herself only the one—and when she'd part from that girl at the end of the school year, she'd still invite her to her house, so that, over the years, there were favorites of all ages whom she taught to prepare a formal tea party, to arrange her table with linens and flowers, with Russian porcelain so thin that light shimmered through the hand-painted violets, the kind of porcelain—the girls felt certain—their mothers and aunts would have locked away from them.

The first with new fashions, Fräulein Siderova would ask her young guests, "How do I look now?"

When she had her reddish-brown hair cut in a bob before other women in the village dared to wear it that style, she asked Michel Abramowitz, the husband of her best friend, Ilse, to take her photo. Michel was not just a lawyer but also an amateur photographer who took pictures of the townspeople in his unique style that considered the background as much as the individual, who was always off to one side, never in the middle.

The photo with the short bob exposed a tiny birthmark on Fräulein Siderova's jaw near her earlobe where her hair used to cover it.

"Like a smudge from a kiss," her girls sighed.

"A kiss from her lover . . ."

They whispered about her oil portrait above her credenza. So romantic, the girls said when she told them it was painted by an artist she'd met aboard a ship on a pilgrimage to Jerusalem. So romantic, how she watched him there from her painting.

*

The old women in town said that during those times when there was an abundance of dying, there was also an abundance of poetry. "As if there ever could be too much poetry," they would say.

Some of the people Sonja Siderova read to were grandparents or parents of her students, even some of her students once they became women and the high fever of childbirth took them. And because she was not frightened of death, she stilled the fear of the dying who had faith in her power to transform their fear by holding it inside her soul, however briefly, before she let it dissipate.

Glass bowls the townspeople gave her, vases that she kept empty to let the light pass through. If needed, they'd fetch her from school to read to their dying, poems that they'd liked as children and that took them back to being children: *playing on the jetties with the froth of river near their ankles . . . or running through forest into that green-white flicker of sun . . . or sledding down the dike through whirls of snowflakes against their cheeks.* Sometimes the dying were afraid of what had been unfinished with a parent, say, or a child, a sibling. In their eyes—especially in the eyes of those who figured they had no secrets—Fräulein Siderova saw their secrets, but she never revealed them because she believed that you held claim to your own secrets.

During her absences from school, her friend, Frau Abramowitz, would often arrive and sketch with the students. She, too, had studied to be a teacher, but she couldn't work as a teacher because she was a married woman now. If she wasn't available, it was assumed that Fräulein Siderova's most accomplished student—like Thekla Jansen in 1912 and Trudi Montag in 1925—would lead her class in memorizing one of the poems she marked for just those absences in her Echtermeyer collection.

*

Occasionally, a new edition of the Echtermeyer was published, but Sonja Siderova continued to teach from the one her parents had bought when they reached Burgdorf the week after her eighth birthday. At home in Russia, higher education had been limited to ten percent of all Jewish children, and Sonja's parents—like many Russian parents who wanted the best education for their children—settled in Germany, where many professors and teachers were Jews and more than a quarter of all Jewish students went on to secondary school. In Germany, the Siderovas felt welcome. They had no idea that the more they'd blend in, the more resentful the townspeople would become of their success and their house and their work and their children's good grades.

Sonja's Echtermeyer had water stains on the linen binding from falling into the Rhein when her father had rowed his wife and children across the fast-moving river one July afternoon to celebrate their arrival in Burgdorf. Skillful at navigating the rented boat past the long freighters, he let them pass before he cut through the current, but the boat wobbled as it reached shore, jammed into the sand, causing Sonja to drop her heavy book of poems into the water. Although the thin pages would dry overnight, the binding would retain the dampness so that, after it had fully dried, the river was still there, brownish ripples against the linen.

"Quite lovely, actually," Sonja's mother said. "Like watermarks on expensive Italian paper."

During their second year in Burgdorf, the Siderova family converted to Catholicism. Some of the parishioners liked to say the Siderovas were *frommer als der Papst*—more pious than the pope. They had eight rosaries, two religious paintings, and a framed photo of the pope; they never missed a Sunday mass, where they prayed with obvious devotion; they liked the rituals and took them on as their own. What the parishioners and the priest didn't know was that the Siderovas distrusted the ritual of confession. They seemed so devout as they knelt in the dim confessional. But all they fed the priest were made-up sins because they suspected all priests disturbed the garden of secrets by tearing at the roots.

*

One morning Fräulein Siderova arrived in her classroom with a stack of books in her arms, and atop the stack a red geranium in a clay pot that she set on the windowsill, red reflected in the glass. Then she had her girls recite the multiplication tables. Whenever they stumbled, she corrected them, gently, made them repeat so that they'd remember from now on.

Suddenly, one of the girls laughed, then another. They were pointing to the window where a butterfly flapped its wings against the outside of the glass as if trying to get to the red geranium. A yellow butterfly. Fluttering away. But coming back.

"What do we know that the butterfly doesn't know?" Fräulein Siderova asked, switching from multiplication to philosophy in an instant.

"That the window is closed."

"The butterfly doesn't know that it can't get through."

Thekla's heart was beating, fast, because that's what it felt like with her *Vati*. If she could find a way to reach him . . . She raised her hand. "Missing someone is like that . . . missing how he might be."

"Oh *ja* . . ." Fräulein Siderova saw inside Thekla's soul, recognized the hoping and the waiting, the maybe and the never again.

The butterfly was beating its wings against the glass.

"That butterfly will never get to the flowers," Gisela said.

"Because it's God's will," Marianne said. "And that makes it fate."

"Actually, what we have here," Fräulein Siderova said, "is a truth. Butterflies cannot fly through glass. Truth?"

"Truth," her girls agreed.

"But within that truth—for us, as humans—there is choice. If you watch closely, you can reach into fate with both arms and affect the outcome."

*

"When I was your age," Thekla tells her boys, "my teacher altered fate for one butterfly." She describes how Fräulein Siderova brought the potted geranium to school, how one butterfly kept returning to the window.

"But then Fräulein Siderova opened the window. She lifted her clay pot with the geranium, set it outside on the brick ledge so the butterfly could reach it. It was part of her teaching . . . that we can alter fate."

Thekla hopes the story of the butterfly will make her boys think. She finds Fräulein Siderova's philosophy more appealing than the church's doctrine that God knows your every thought, that without God's plan no sparrow falls from a tree. Or is it the sky? A barn? So much of religion is like politics—coercion and superstitious non-sense. At the university, Thekla read Darwin's *Die Entstehung der Arten,* and she has been teaching her boys about evolution without naming it that. To her, evolution makes for a more sophisticated God.

When Franz and Walter raise their hands, she's ready for their questions.

Chapter 10

"WHEN IS FRÄULEIN Siderova coming back?" Franz asks.

"Never," Walter says.

"Yes, she is," Richard insists.

"She's a *Jude,*" Andreas says. "That's why she can't come back."

Thekla flinches. During her first month of teaching, she was afraid Fräulein Siderova would come back, and she felt ashamed at her relief that the school couldn't restore the position to a Jewish teacher.

"I lost my teacher in fourth grade, just like you," she tells her boys. "She went to America with her new husband, to help him bring up his three children. Their mothers had died during childbirth."

Suddenly her boys are solemn. Nearly every family has a mother or aunt or sister in the cemetery from giving birth. *Giving death.* They know that's how women can die. Or lose all sanity if their babies changed into dwarfs like Trudi Montag. If you dropped babies, their heads got big, but not their bodies. You, too, could change into a dwarf, stop growing altogether if you didn't clean your ears or if you didn't say your prayers or if you ate butter with a spoon or if you lied to your parents or if you broke your sister's doll. And once you were a dwarf, you were a dwarf forever.

*

"Let me show you where in America my teacher lives now." Thekla Jansen picks up the pointer, moves it to America on the map of the world. "After she left, we met our new teacher."

"Our Fräulein Siderova."

Thekla nods. "She was my Fräulein Siderova, too."

"But when is she coming back to us?" Eckart Holthusen wants to know.

Do they wish they had you here instead, Fräulein Siderova? Do they think I betrayed you? Because I did. No, I didn't. Because what else could I have done?

Her boys are waiting.

"Soon we liked Fräulein Siderova as much as Fräulein Montag, who married and went to America. I was at her wedding."

"In America?"

"No no, the wedding was in Burgdorf. She invited our whole class."

"Will you invite us to your wedding?" Otto can see Fräulein Jansen in her wedding gown, white lace and a veil and white flowers. . . .

Franz giggles.

But the others want her the way she is. There's something girl-wild about her, and yet she doesn't look down on boys like regular girls. On her, they can practice how to treat girls.

Two of their mothers—Frau Weskopp and Frau Beil—have told the teacher their sons have become more polite. Some of her boys she understands better than their parents do. Because she listens to them, encourages them. Already, she can picture them as men. She'll encounter them in church or at the pharmacy or on the street. Some will visit her on Sunday afternoons with flowers, say, or on certain occasions, like Christmas, perhaps Mother's Day. They'll come to her with stories about their work and their own children, tell her how lovely she is. *Men. But for her always boys.*

She smiles mysteriously. "You don't want me to get married."

But Otto is still thinking of her in that white gown. "Why not?"

"Because as a teacher I can help more children than if I were a mother. And if I got married, I'd have to stop being your teacher. I couldn't do that, could I?"

They shake their heads. They'd be devastated if she were to let one man displace them. *Boys. They all have crushes on her.*

*

Last Saturday, when Thekla danced with Emil Hesping through the blue-warm haze of tobacco smoke in Potter's bar, her palm was against his chest, and his white shirt felt so insubstantial that she wanted her hand on that muscle without the shirt. That's how the wanting always started for her, with that rough, immediate pull. Skin, breath, voice—coming at her all at once.

"I think more than ever the Nazis framed that crazy Dutch communist," he said.

"Not so loud," she warned.

"They set the Reichstag on fire and lured the poor Dutchman in there so that they could blame communist terrorists . . . seize KPD buildings and weapons, get emergency powers."

"Enough—"

"You're too careful." Emil spun her past a whirl of uniforms and suits, past brown shirts and armbands. "They want to convince us that the communists were stockpiling weapons for a revolution."

"Must you distort everything?"

"Distort? As a teacher you should be appalled at how *they* distort language."

She pressed her forehead against his mouth to stop him from talking.

His lips and voice against her skin: about how Hitler claimed to have protected the German people not just from devious enemies and known dangers but also from dangers he couldn't reveal for their own protection; about how the sheep of Germany were so grateful to Hitler that they were trading their freedom for that illusion.

"Don't you ever question how involved the Führer was in the fire?" Emil asked.

"Enough," she said.

"Whenever I think, now he has gone too far, now we'll surely get rid of him, he steps up his audacity."

"I'm not going to listen to this," she said. It was enough that he went to secret meetings of the KPD, Kommunistische Partei Deutschlands, though it was forbidden. She wished he were more discreet, like Herr Abramowitz, who also was a communist.

"When he talks about freedom, he means national freedom, not individual freedom. Don't you see—"

"You'll get us arrested."

"I'm too fast for the *braunen Halunken*—brown goons." *Emil. Irreverent. Exciting. Dangerous.*

He kissed her forehead, and when she pulled away, he laughed, and his black eyebrows drew together above the bridge of his wonderfully curved nose till they joined into one brow. She loved that contrast to his smooth, bald head. As a girl she'd thought men's hair grew lower with age so that, once they were dreadfully old, it was all between their toes. All her life she'd seen Emil around town. He was twenty-five when she was ten and watched him at a competition, gliding on the trapeze above her like a sorcerer. And now that she was thirty-four, he was forty-nine and more limber than men her age.

"You can't possibly believe the blind Dutchman did it."

*

The Dutchman. Marinus. Marinus van der Lubbe. More like a boy than a man in newspaper photos, with his round face and wide lips and those dazed, dazed eyes, the rim of his cap so low on his forehead that shadows leaked below his eyes like those painted triangles below the eyes of a clown. Thekla usually fell for the sullen type, worked herself inside out to evoke a smile, a response.

Some said the Dutchman was bare-chested and ranting when they captured him inside the Reichstag. Half-naked, others said, wielding a torch, sweat beading on his chest. Yet, in the newspaper Marinus van der Lubbe was no longer bare-chested but subdued in a jacket buttoned high over his shirt. One photo showed him with the translator who was assigned to him.

"He was not blind," Thekla told Emil.

"Blind enough to be incapable of burning down that huge mess of a building."

"Fräulein Siderova said he was three quarters blind."

"Fräulein Siderova still speaks to you?"

Thekla flinched.

"I'm sorry, *Liebchen*."

"I've never taken anything from Fräulein Siderova. No matter what people say."

Emil pulled her close.

Thekla has looked for Fräulein Siderova in the church choir, but she hasn't been there since last spring. She's seen her only once, at the Christmas mass, in a pew near the exit, not upstairs with the choir where she belonged, singing Handel's *Messiah* with Trudi Montag and the taxidermist and Frau Weskopp and the pharmacist and the other members.

"The last time I was in Düsseldorf," she said, "I bought another present for her. A small box made of blue glass. I do that whenever I see something she might like. If I can afford it, I buy it for her, and when I visit her—"

"What I adore about you . . ." He pulled her closer yet. " . . . is that impossibly high upper lip of yours, but especially that little groove above it."

"Philtrum. That's what the old Greeks called it."

"Why must the Greeks always be old?"

"They considered it to be the most sensual part of the body. Their word for it was *philtrum. Liebeszauber*—love magic."

"And is it?" With his thumb, he skimmed that sweet ridge between her nose and her upper lip, and felt her mouth quiver. How sensual she was. He adored that about her, that and her quick intelligence. She would make a good chess player.

*

"You would make a good chess player," he said.

She felt his heat throughout her body, down to the hidden flesh behind her knees. She stumbled. Swayed. "I'm already a good chess player."

"We should play, then." He swayed with her.

And she knew she wanted to go home with him. Tonight.

He said, "So there is a name for it . . . philtrum. I was told it's where my guardian angel pressed one finger before I was born. To make me forget the secret I knew from before birth."

"Some babies are born without a philtrum," she said, "the skin there flat. Does that mean your guardian angels don't touch those babies with the secret? And that therefore, they'll remember the secret?"

Emil thought of the third Heidenreich girl—a woman of twenty but forever a girl—Gerda, with her flat upper lip, her crazy lurch of a walk. Unsteady, mind and body. And yet, Gerda could pass for pretty when she sat without motion, without words, on the front steps of her father's taxidermy shop.

"You don't believe in angels," Thekla said abruptly.

"Stories. I believe in stories."

"So who told you *that* story?"

"A wise woman."

"What's her name?"

"She said the secret is always inside us, but we won't remember it till we die. If we knew the secret, we'd be blinded by it."

"What's your wise woman's name?"

"You . . ." He laughed aloud. " . . . are jealous!"

"I don't believe in being jealous."

"Not believing isn't enough to keep it away." He grazed her lips with his. "Duck lips."

"Your reputation for flattery is unsurpassed."

"That bad?"

"That bad."

"Child lips then?" Emil. Against her. Hard. "Think of the timing! One week before the elections. How convenient. And Hitler had the audacity to claim the fire was a signal from God."

*

They danced past Maria Bertels, who was sitting with two brownshirts, coarse, boisterous, definitely not the kind of men Thekla would go out with. What was Maria doing with them?

She glanced away when Thekla waved to her. Probably because she was still at Henkel's in Düsseldorf, waiting for a teaching job. It cut through Thekla, that familiar uneasiness—having while others didn't. At the university, she and Maria used to belong to the hiking club, and after they'd graduated, they continued to hike with others from the club, dancing at the *Karneval,* sharing frugal dinners, complaining that there were no teaching positions because of the peace treaty and reparation costs.

Until last spring, they'd been friends, as long as Thekla, too, was working any dismal job just to keep *Leib und Seele zusammen*—body and soul together: clerk in an optician's shop, at a lumberyard, in a pharmacy, when she could have done so much more with her education. The humiliation of losing even those jobs. And always that doubt: *If I'm not a teacher, then who am I?* Private lessons barely paid, but Fräulein Siderova said they would make Thekla feel like a teacher. And they did. Just as the visits to Fräulein Siderova's classroom made Thekla feel like a teacher. For that hour. That half day. Making it excruciating to return to work that was not teaching. Many of her classmates were still in jobs like Maria's and hadn't taught at all.

*

Thekla longed for a friendship with a woman. Like the friendship of Sonja Siderova and Ilse Abramowitz. Every Sunday, the two women took long walks by the Rhein, as had been their custom for decades. From a distance, they were like sisters, tall and swift as they leaned their bodies into the wind and talked. Always talked.

They must know everything about one another.

But they revealed nothing. Especially not what happened to Ilse Abramowitz's first child. The people of Burgdorf said the child must have been born dead or had died right after birth. Yet, there was no marker for a child on the Abramowitzes' family plot. That's why the old widows, who rode their bicycles to the cemetery to tend their families' graves, suspected that Ilse Abramowitz had started bleeding on the train, that the trembling of steel wheels against steel rails must have initiated the trembling of her womb. What the widows knew for sure were these facts: One morning in the fall of 1899, a very pregnant Frau Abramowitz had climbed aboard the 8:42 train, accompanied by Sonja Siderova; but two days later, when the two returned, Ilse Abramowitz's belly was flat, absolutely flat—without that gentle swelling most women retain for weeks after giving birth—and Sonja Siderova had to support her elbow as though she were an invalid. For weeks Ilse

Abramowitz cried, wouldn't look people in the face, but since she didn't speak of any miscarriage, it would have been ill-mannered to ask.

After that first pregnancy, it took her four years to conceive again, long enough for people to speculate that she'd never have children; but then she had two in a row, first her daughter, Ruth, and the following summer her son, Albert, and when she'd go for her walks with Fräulein Siderova, one would be pushing the wicker carriage, the other the stroller.

*

Maybe, Thekla thought, she could form a friendship like theirs with Gisela. As girls, they'd played together. And Gisela likes it that her son's teacher lives upstairs. Maybe they—

"Four thousand arrests!" Emil. Still going on about the communists and intellectuals who were arrested that night. "That list was ready before. The arrests happened so quickly. Think of who benefited."

Him, she'd make wait. There was something delicious in waiting for what you could have now, prolonging your anticipation. Delicious. If waiting was what *you* chose—not what the priest chose for you.

Emil reeled her against his body. "That mass obedience . . . I've seen it at the sports club, the attitude that they've given up rights for the greater good. They feel justified in demanding we all make the same sacrifice, and—"

"Not so loud."

"—they get indignant when we don't. It reminds them of what they've given up."

"Tonight you'll sleep alone again," she murmured.

*

Emil tilted his head to hear better, felt her palm against his chest as she pressed herself away from him, danced away from him, lithe, graceful, danced for herself, Thekla, not with him, eyes hooded, no smile, danced for herself only, nothing flowing around her, not even her hair, cap of black locks, dress sculpted to her so that her body beneath the fabric was all he saw as she danced, not seeing him in that dance where he couldn't retrieve her into his arms as she came up against him because she retreated again, and he nothing but a body she needed across from her so she could do this in public, because to sway like that alone would be indecent, and tonight he was that body—it could be anyone for her—tomorrow some other man, dancing with her but not reaching her, aching to kiss those long eyelids, those upturned lips—duck lips, child lips—parted as if to ask something of him that he could never give her because she wouldn't tell him what it was; and yet, yet, this dancing for herself only made her more seductive, inviting without welcoming him, and as he danced across from her, he found—for an instant—his reflection in her pupils, black pupils with those golden-brown rims, but his image couldn't enter her, just flitted on the surface—he for himself, not for her—which would never be enough for him. While for her it was. As she danced. Swayed.

1900

Chapter 11

When Almut Jansen was hired to keep house for a stonecutter, she couldn't bring Thekla along, and it stunned her how deeply she missed this baby she hadn't wanted till recently. The practical solution was to let her mother-in-law bring Thekla with her to work at the St. Margaret Home and settle her in the nursery.

But practical is not necessarily good for the soul. Almut knew her mother-in-law would visit Thekla throughout the day in the nursery, just as she had her own son; but it chafed at Almut to imagine her daughter with those children in limbo, whose loneliness showed in their desperate eagerness whenever you walked toward them, and in their dispiritedness once they saw that you were not coming for them. The older these children got, the less likely they were to be adopted, and a few months before starting first grade, they were transferred to the orphanage in Husum.

Almut couldn't bear to have Thekla think of herself as one of these children without family; and when her former employer offered to hire her back, she asked Wilhelm about moving to Burgdorf. "I could bring Thekla with me to work."

"But how about the man who—?"

"You said you didn't want to know."

"Going to Burgdorf makes it different . . . if that's where he lives."

"I have nothing left for him. Nothing."

Wilhelm opened his lips. Closed them.

She told him that she was no longer drawn to the child's father, that she knew too much about him. His habits. The hairs on his brush. His distance from his wife.

"He is married?" Wilhelm was startled. And immediately relieved.

"It has all gone to you now, that love," she said, "to you and to Thekla. I'll never touch him again."

Wilhelm felt uneasy. But he also knew that the people of Nordstrand would never forget that Almut had married him while pregnant with another man's child. Burgdorf she had left *before* anyone knew of her disgrace, and she could return there proudly, a married woman with her husband and child.

"They need toymakers in Burgdorf," Almut told him. "There are so many of you here."

He nodded. So many that it seemed he'd always be one of the new toymakers, no matter what his age, working on the crowded main floor instead of upstairs in the design studio where he longed to be.

"Go to Burgdorf," his mother told him.

"You don't want me to stay?"

"Here, they will always gossip."

Almut stroked her mother-in-law's arm from the wrist up to the elbow and back again, and she felt her shiver. "I wish you'd come with us."

"Yes," Wilhelm said. "We want you to come with us."

"I know you do," Lotte told them. "But—"

"They need midwives in Burgdorf, too," he said.

"Midwives and toymakers . . . I can't leave here."

"But you'll visit?" Thekla asked.

"Christmas. You'll come to me in the summer."

*

Wilhelm was accustomed to the sound of the sea at high tide and the absolute stillness at low tide, but in Burgdorf his wife taught him to listen to the murmur of the river that you could hear from anywhere in her village, at any hour, a constant murmur that touched upon her lifeblood. He could see that this village was as much a part of his wife as the shape of her face and her long neck. Here in the Rheinland everyone talked in her melodic dialect. Here, she could be joyful with their daughter, promenade her around town in a wicker carriage.

Alexander Sturm hired Wilhelm as a master carver. Though the toy factory had every tool a toymaker might desire, Wilhelm used only the tools he'd brought with him from Nordstrand, and he never had to replace a single tool because he kept them meticulously cleaned and oiled.

The factory made jumping-jacks and spinning tops and stuffed lambs and—the owner's favorite—fairy-tale building blocks that fit into puzzles, six sides to each block, nine blocks to each puzzle, that Wilhelm Jansen carved with infinitesimal scenes from *"Aschenputtel"*—"Cinderella," "Rapunzel," *"Froschkönig"*—"Frog King," *"Schneewitchen"*—"Snow White," and other fairy tales. If you didn't fit those blocks together as they were intended, they'd form strange tales that could make you laugh or cry out or ponder the twists in your own life.

*

Every noon, after the Abramowitzes had eaten, Almut would ladle the rest of the food she'd prepared in their kitchen into pots with lids that she'd stack inside a pail because the pots were hot to the touch. It embarrassed Wilhelm when he walked home for his mid-day meal and came upon his wife carrying his meal in a pail. *Hog slop?* He felt petty. Reminded himself how eagerly she loved him at night. What an accomplished cook she was. How she anticipated his hungers and kept his clothes clean. How she noticed the chafing of his trousers against the insides of his thighs and sponged him with a tincture she boiled from chamomile. How she served meat more often than their neighbors because the lawyer Abramowitz could afford it. Still, whatever his wife served him came after the lawyer had eaten his fill.

As Wilhelm dreamed of toys he wanted to make, he tried to reassemble the stories of his own life the way they were given to him at birth, building blocks of one mother and one father and four children, and how those blocks—scattered underwater—were still unsettling the blocks of his own family. With Almut, he had believed he could fit these blocks together, make the picture whole, but his daughter's likeness to the lawyer Abramowitz was disturbing the pattern, though Wilhelm fought knowing for sure, fought the inertia by reminding himself what mattered was his own devotion to the girl. *Thekla.* Always at him with her adoration, her curiosity, till he gave in to her, let her careen with him toward the tilted sea, where direction was no more than something to fall away from, where nothing but his daughter's voice, her hands, could lure him back. *Thekla.* Her fierce tug on his fingers when she learned to walk. *Thekla.* Right at his elbow when he built a box for his tools, dismantling twelve cigar boxes that Leo Montag had saved for him at the pay-library and assembling them into one double-layered box that he sanded and lacquered with Chinese red. He let Thekla choose the color. After he nailed brass reinforcements on all corners, he didn't have to carve his name into the front panel because no other toymaker in Burgdorf and the surrounding villages owned a toolbox that magnificent.

One morning, as he carved the blocks for *"Rumpelstilzchen,"* he had an image of his wife peeling potatoes in the lawyer's kitchen, sunlight on her hands and on the long curlicue peels while she spun golden spirals like the miller's daughter, who was forced to spin straw into pure gold.

Tuesday, February 27, 1934

Chapter 12

THE TAXIDERMIST ALWAYS gets dachshunds, and he—"

"He stuffs his dead ones."

"If you ask him, he lets you pet them."

"And then he—"

Fräulein Jansen's students are giggling like six-year-olds.

"And then he buys a new one, a live one, and—"

"And . . . and he introduces the live one to the stuffed ones."

"No."

"It's true."

"Once he gave me a glass eye."

"When I was your age," the teacher says, "the taxidermist gave glass eyes to the children of Burgdorf on St. Martin's Day, not sweets or apples like other merchants when we came to his shop with our paper lanterns. Those eyes . . ." She rolls her eyes, makes the boys laugh. "Actually, I liked getting those eyes."

"Did you use them as marbles?" Andreas asks.

"Oh yes."

"Because that's what my father did with them."

"We have three of those eyes," Eckart Holthusen says. "They're painted over in back of the glass."

The teacher nods. Taps her left ear to remind him.

Eckart winces. Pulls his finger from his ear and hides both hands on his knees.

Slack manners, she thinks. Everyone in the Holthusen family has slack manners. Eckart's mother. His grandmother. Two women raising one boy. Whenever his mother cleans St. Martin's Church, the sharp odor of her sweat hangs in the vestibule for hours after. The parishioners know to stay away when she lifts her broom to get at the cobwebs above the confessionals, say, or the ceilings of the side altars. Keeping the church clean but not herself. That stickiness of body secretions. Armpits. Ears. And worse. Some parishioners say it's because she carries her mother's sin. Being born out of wedlock will mark a family for generations, so that even grandchildren will feel dirty by the way others treat them.

*

Eckart wishes he could lay his head on the desk and shut his eyes. Last night he awoke crying again, his ear tight and hot. His *Mutti* got him up, took him into the kitchen, where she filled a spoon with cooking oil and held it above the stove. When it was warm, she soaked a shred of *Watte*—cotton in the oil. He knew what came next, cocked his head to the right so that his left ear was up and *Mutti* could stick in the *Watte*. Some drops trickled deeper than the *Watte* could go, making him shiver and swallow as they warmed up the pain, shrinking its edges.

He slept, then, while *Mutti* sat by his bed. But this morning the cotton was little and so deep inside his ear that his mother couldn't pull it out with her fingernails or her tweezer, and she said she'd take him to Frau Doktor Rosen today after school.

*

"Bruno's family never gets the same kind of dog," Franz says.

"Because they're so ugly that there is no same kind." Wolfgang tap-taps one finger against Bruno's back.

Bruno jerks away from him, draws into himself as far as he can, elbows tight against his sides.

"Wolfgang," the teacher warns.

But he persists, one finger tap-tapping down Bruno's spine. Maybe tomorrow he'll tie Bruno's shoelaces together again. So easy to get him flustered.

"Stop it!" The veins in Bruno's skinny neck stick out.

"Your last dog was fuzzy with a tail like a pig," Eckart joins in.

"It will make you so happy to know my last dog got trampled dead."

"Not happy," Eckart protests.

"By the ragman's horse. But the day after, a spotted dog came to our door, and I named her Henrietta."

"Henrietta was lucky to find Bruno," the teacher says. "Right, boys?" But her eyes are on Wolfgang.

Wolfgang nods, folds his hands on his desk. Once, in the barbershop, he heard his uncle say that the Stosicks got only ugly dogs—the kind that come from two mismatched breeds getting stuck to each other—and Wolfgang pictured a dog with two heads and two tails, one set at each end, so that it could run in both directions.

*

During recess, several boys breathe against the ice-flowers and ice-stems, nudging one another aside, melting larger circles that remind them of something Fräulein has told them: once a hole opens in how you've been looking at the world, everything else pushes through. Beyond their breaths, dormant wisteria vines twist around the window. In the school yard, the fruit trees are bare.

All grown and bare now, the teacher thinks, as she steps behind the boys and rests her hands on Richard's bony shoulders. Such a heavy head on a slight neck. Such a burden . . . She wishes she could do more for Richard. Some people still cross the street to avoid an illegitimate child or the woman who's borne that child.

Around the fruit trees the ground is still frozen, and a timid sun casts its peculiar light on the hoarfrost, illuminating and devouring at once. When Fräulein Siderova planted these trees with her students one long-ago May—one pear, one apple, one plum—they were knee-high on Thekla.

Chapter 13

"YOUR BIRTHDAY," Thekla Jansen says to her students, "is the anniversary of the day you were born. And don't we look forward to those anniversaries?"

"To getting a present," says Andreas, who wants to be a policeman.

"Every day has an anniversary attached to it," she says, "but the ones we remember are those that transformed us." Just then a reckless thought comes at her— *When you shake out the night, this is what falls out—*

Just as it came at her last April when she saw the Führer at a huge rally in Düsseldorf. He didn't know how to speak properly, how to walk properly, how to comb his hair, and she felt embarrassed for him as he shouted about restoring jobs and national honor, about a better and splendid Germany. The mob applauded, shouted. Did people really believe that he wanted what was best for Germany? That history would prove he was on the good side? When the Führer was a boy—Thekla was sure of that—no one taught him how to conduct himself. If Fräulein Siderova had been his teacher, he would have learned to stand tall but not rigidly, to pace his voice along with his breath instead of letting it flare into hysteria.

At the edge of the crowd, a child was trying to leave. Thekla couldn't make out who it was, only that people were making space for someone short who was moving against the thrust of the crowd. But it wasn't a child, Thekla finally saw. It was Trudi Montag from the Burgdorf pay-library. Thekla wanted to follow her, get out of there with her; but just then a cheer soared from the masses as the Führer reached into the sea of bodies and plucked a little girl from her mother's arms—there must have been hundreds of children thrust at him by adults—and lifted her higher yet, a girl with blond braids, too high. Some felt an odd sense of alarm, and they'd think it was because he might drop the girl, because he was that awkward, but when he lowered her into her mother's arms and picked another child, they shook off that warning.

*

When you shake out the night—

Thekla Jansen sets one index finger against her lips to keep herself from saying it aloud to her boys: *When you shake out the night, this is what falls out.*

And to think that some say the Führer is Germany's savior.

Messages change. Right and wrong can trade places, fall out of fashion.

As a student teacher she was assigned to a school in Neuss, where children—as was the custom, and to teach them to obey—were punished with a quick slap on the cheek for whispering in class, say, or with a ruler on their fingers if they didn't sit still. When Thekla was a child, she, too, was punished like that. Sister Elisabeth used to grasp the shell of a student's ear between her fingers, twist it, and Thekla dreaded that ear-twist more than a slap or the ruler.

But one morning, when Thekla was the one to snap her ruler

across the knuckles of a small boy, she suddenly knew it was wrong, knew it in her bones and in her gut. Punishment wasn't effective in guiding a child toward learning. Far more effective to bind a child to you with devotion so that it longed to follow your teaching. From that day forward, she decided, she would teach according to her own moral compass.

And that's becoming more important now.

She knows how to adapt, even to the fear that has been pulling the people together ever since the Reichstag burned. No longer the splintering of many groups. No longer the humiliation of Versailles. Instead: unity, a half-remembered pride. What matters to her is that her boys are thriving. The rest she'll wait out.

But Emil doesn't grasp the complexity.

"It's not about enthusiasm for the Nazis, only enthusiasm for what they can do for my students," she told him two weekends ago, when they were riding their bicycles to Düsseldorf to eat in the Altstadt.

"And how do you separate that?"

He was in an argumentative mood, told her his gymnasts' club had lost two more athletes to the SA sports club. Already his official membership was low because Jews were excluded from sports clubs.

"But I let them train before dawn," he told her.

"I don't want to know that." She pedaled faster, swerved ahead of him.

"You would do the same," he shouted after her.

*

A truck rumbles past the schoolhouse, the pigeons scatter, and in that flicker of motion and light, the students raise their heads, sniffing blood though there is no blood, not yet, only this truck with animals in back, heading for the slaughterhouse. Used to be only carts that delivered animals there, but more trucks now, modern and fast.

Their rabbits and chickens people kill in their backyards where the ground soaks up blood. But pigs and cattle get hauled to the slaughterhouse, eyes rolling white in their sockets, seeking you inside your nightmares with squealing that sounds human.

Enough—

Corn for the pigeons, Thekla reminds herself. They're like beggars, always hungry, scavenging. If she were to hold one in her hands, it would squirm—dirty and warm, scrawny, not sleek and pampered like the pigeons her *Vater* used to raise in the coop on the flat part of their roof. Suddenly she misses them.

*

As a child, she used to climb the stairs to the roof early in the morning, whenever *Vati* was at the asylum in Grafenberg. A few kernels on her shoulders, she'd wait for the tamest birds, Aphrodite and Zeus, wait for the luscious quiver of wings against her throat and ears, that guttural echo from deep within their feather-breasts. Only then would she toss corn to the other pigeons.

Evenings she'd sweep the wooden floorboards of their coop and refill their drinking water while they'd preen and strut for her. The year she was seven, *Vati* told her the legends of the gods who inspired the names for his pigeons.

Athena . . . Poseidon . . . Eris . . .

That was when he still climbed from his darkness for a month, say, or a few days, and those hands of his could build anything: the pigeon coop, a cupboard, planters. Wednesday evenings he'd let Thekla stay up late—not her little brothers, just Thekla—and walk with her to the Burgdorf *Tauben Klub*—pigeon club, where he was president for almost three months.

Artemis . . . Hebe . . . Eros . . .

Some of them eaten. Pigeon soup *Mutti* cooked when there was nothing else. Pigeon stew. Insignificant, the meat, once you separated it from feather and bone. But the best racers *Vati* saved for breeding.

Hestia . . . Apollo . . . Dionysus . . .

Thekla's first poem was about a Racing Homer, Athena. Frau Abramowitz wrote it down for her because she was five, could tell the poem, not write it. Athena flew out of her father's head. That's where babies came from. Athena flew across the Rhein, carrying an olive tree for her Uncle Poseidon. A wolf caught Athena. But she flew away and hid in a house with three beds. One small, one medium, one big. Athena slept in every bed. Then she ate the pudding. The End.

*

Thekla smiles to herself. That poem . . . it came from everywhere, from legends and fairy tales and superstitions, and from what surrounded her. All equally real. She enjoys that age when everything is still equally real for children, that age before they believe grown-ups who'll tell them what's real and what's not. If Thekla were given a choice, she'd ask to teach first graders, because for them it's still all real.

"Fräulein?" Heinz says and then adds something she can't make out because it's in his Bavarian dialect.

But she's pleased he's speaking at all. Only two weeks ago his family moved here, and he's been quiet in her classroom, as if *Hochdeutsch*—High German were a foreign language for him.

How would you get him to engage, Fräulein Siderova? Be patient? Nudge him with encouragement? He seems to understand much of what I say but can't express himself.

I wish I could visit you, bring you one of the gifts I've been collecting for you. Maybe the little glass figure of the ballerina that'll remind you of taking ballet lessons as a girl in Russia? I can almost feel it in my hand. My hand inside my coat pocket as I walk toward your apartment. But the closer I get, the more nervous I am. I slow my steps. Stop at Alexander Sturm's new apartment building. When I reach Schlosserstrasse 78, I stand on the street below your bay window. I ring the bell, climb the steps into the mint smell that started with one plant I gave you. You separated the new shoots, giving them to others in your building until every landing had a pottery box with mint on the windowsill. You open your door, lift the glass ballerina to the light, admire her profile, unadorned and graceful. "Oh, Thekla," you say and set it on the glass shelf in your flower window. "How exquisite."

The smell of mint—

*

—so strong that Thekla is startled to be standing in her classroom.

Too soon—

Too soon to come to you, Fräulein Siderova.

"Heinz?" She takes a step toward the desk where he sits next to Otto, in the space that used to be Markus's.

Quickly, he glances down, hides his eyes behind hair that's longer than the other students'.

"The way I talk," she whispers to him, "must sound funny to you."

He covers his mouth. Giggles behind his palm. He's far too thin. She can tell it's from hunger, not his build: wrists and elbows too large for his arms, sunken cheeks.

If I can teach my Vater, *I can teach anyone. When skin becomes speech. Language. Words. And I the translator.*

Yet, how much lost in the translation? Marinus van der Lubbe had a translator. A photo of them together in the paper, the young Dutchman not looking one bit like an arsonist, but rather innocent and a bit sullen. He was used to being poor: a father who left after Marinus was born, an accident at a jobsite that kept Marinus from continuing as a bricklayer, an invalid's pension.

If Marinus had been your student, Fräulein Siderova, he would have known how to handle himself in public. If only all the boys of the world could come to you for their education, they would grow up to be polite and kind. Dress and behave to their advantage. No bullies.

1903
September

Chapter 14

FRAU ABRAMOWITZ TOOK the fairy-tale book from a shelf, sat at the gleaming table, and lifted Thekla onto her lap. Her dress was cool against Thekla's arm, and yet it smelled hot, that familiar smell of *Mutti*'s hot iron and starch and Henkel's bleaching soda. Thekla made herself be quiet, well mannered, while Frau Abramowitz read to her about Dornröschen, who was cursed by a wicked fairy. But three good fairies changed the curse from death into a long, long sleep. A sleep of a hundred years before a prince rescued Dornröschen with his kiss.

"Just like this," Frau Abramowitz said and kissed Thekla's cheek. "Ask if you want anything. Anything at all."

What is anything at all? Chocolate cigarettes? A pony? Thekla's heart was bumping. She'd never stayed in the Abramowitzes' house without *Mutti*.

"You're my beautiful girl," Frau Abramowitz said.

Everything the Abramowitzes had was beautiful. Beautiful pillows. Beautiful windows. Beautiful books. Beautiful fruit not bruised by falling, or by time. And now she was Frau Abramowitz's beautiful girl.

Thekla pointed to the fancy doll on top of the glass cabinet. "Can I play with your doll?"

"That's a carving of St. Anthony of Padua. He's the patron saint of all we've lost. . . ."

"Can I play with your saint?"

Frau Abramowitz stood up and handed him to Thekla. "Sonja Siderova gave him to me. She must think I need a Catholic saint." Then she unlocked her cabinet and took out three photo albums. She had an entire row of albums, a separate one for each faraway place.

Thekla held on to the wooden saint when they sat on the sofa, where Frau Abramowitz spread out her albums and opened thick pages with pictures—elephants and palaces and birds—held in place by black photo corners.

"Venezuela." Frau Abramowitz pointed to one.

Then to another. "Venice."

When Thekla tried out both names, Frau Abramowitz taught her how to pronounce them. She was always teaching Thekla something.

"Someday you'll travel the world, too," she said. "Just wait."

Wait? But then how come *Mutti* said Frau Abramowitz didn't know about waiting? "That woman doesn't know about waiting," *Mutti* had said, "she buys it right away. But even she cannot buy everything she wants."

*

After Frau Abramowitz locked her albums away and positioned her saint back on top of the cabinet, she took Thekla's hand in hers and walked with her to the post office to mail a letter, then to the grocery store to buy groceries for lunch.

At the pay-library, Herr Montag told Frau Abramowitz, "I've been saving a special book for you."

Her face turned pink. "Thank you."

On the cover of the book a doctor and a nurse leaned toward each other across a bed. In the bed lay a man who had bandages all around his body and forehead.

The earache sound of piano music came through the wall.

Frau Abramowitz shook her head. "No one plays like your father."

Herr Montag winced. "Let's be grateful for that."

Thekla was allowed to carry the library book across the street to the Abramowitzes' house, where Herr Abramowitz was already home from his law office, reading the newspaper.

"I understand you're here by yourself today," he said.

She ran to him, inhaled the scent of his pipe, cherries and smoke. "*Mutti* went with *Vati* to his doctor."

"In Grafenberg," Herr Abramowitz said.

Thekla pretended to read the back of his newspaper. Waited for him to see her read.

And then he did. And nodded. "It makes me happy that you're visiting me."

She knew that was true. Because it made him happy to visit her house. After those visits there was always something she hadn't had before: new shoes, watercolors, toys, a white *Himmelbettchen*—canopy bed. Though she liked his gifts, they made her feel odd—*being poor but looking rich*—setting her apart not only from her family but from other families on the block. Yet, it was here that it started, the sense that she deserved more than others, and with it the uneasiness that they envied her.

*

At the table that *Mutti* had polished, Thekla sat with the Abramowitzes and chewed with her mouth closed. She knew how to. And how to stop her feet from banging against the legs of her chair. Now the Abramowitzes could see how nice it was to have a child who ate and played quietly. Who didn't get food on her face.

Frau Abramowitz showed her to keep her elbows and wrists off the table. "Like that, remember?" she asked, gently. "Proper manners will help you through any situation. They're like safety straps in a streetcar. You can always hold on if the streetcar rattles along."

"What if you are too little to reach the straps?" Herr Abramowitz asked and winked at Thekla.

Frau Abramowitz tilted her chin toward him. "Then we'll have to adjust the straps . . . bring them to *your* level."

He puckered his lips. "Amusing."

"I'm good at amusing myself."

After lunch Thekla took her nap in the guest room, where she often napped while *Mutti* cleaned up in the kitchen. Except *Mutti* wasn't here. On the white bed she soon fell asleep to the sound of Herr Abramowitz's telephone voice in the living room—not all quiet-gone like *Vati*'s voice.

But when she woke up, Herr Abramowitz's voice was gone, too. She slid from the mattress and ran into the living room to find him. Only sun, here, yellow on the walls. Yellow on the shelf with his cameras. Yellow on her eyelids and her hair. Yellow on the wood panels as tall as she. Yellow on the telephone. Sometimes neighbors asked to use the telephone, and the Abramowitzes always said yes. If Thekla had a telephone, she would let her neighbors use it, too. Tracing one finger along the top edge of the panels, she followed her finger, pretending the house with its shining parquet floors and Persian carpets belonged to her. She stopped. Sniffed the harsh smell of old tobacco. Above her hung a pipe rack, too high for her to touch. Pinching her nostrils shut, she swirled away from the smell, one swirl, two, three—

On the piano bench lay the pay-library book, its cellophane cover taped in the space between the nurse's mouth and the doctor's mouth. Thekla's *Mutti* liked to say Frau Abramowitz read trash. "All that book learning and refinement, and that woman reads trash."

The piano was like the wing of a stork . . . white, curved. On top a glass bowl with grapes. Miniature frames with photos. Of many Abramowitzes now and long ago. When Thekla touched the grapes, they were like water, green and light. She saw herself setting them into *Vati*'s hands and following him to a place all green and light. It was about reaching him through touch, about shifting his empty hands on his knees so the palms curved up and could hold slippery mud, a sun-baked rock, a scratchy sponge, a sieve. Different textures and temperatures. Then she'd draw pictures of what brought him back into his eyes.

*

If only Frau Abramowitz were awake. Thekla would ask her if she could eat a grape. Frau Abramowitz would say yes. Thekla could almost taste the grape. Climbing onto the bench, she plucked one grape from its stem. Green, it tasted so green that she ate another. She glanced toward the stairway. Still quiet. Another grape yet, and with it a bliss and belonging. Till the ends of most stems were jagged.

And I didn't ask. Didn't—

Steps in the hallway above. Quickly, Thekla lifted the bunch of grapes, rotated it till the ugly stems were underneath—not as high as before, the bunch, *oh*—tugged here, there, rotated the bowl. Fled to the white bed. Pulled the cover to her mouth when Frau Abramowitz came in. Her belly felt sick. Her belly and legs and throat. *What did I do wrong? Is it stealing . . . eating grapes without asking?*

All afternoon, she felt anxious. This was how it was going to happen: Frau Abramowitz would lift the bunch of grapes. Find the empty stems. Now she would never let Thekla come back here.

At dinner, Thekla couldn't swallow. Her tongue felt prickly. Her tongue and also where she swallowed, down inside.

"What is it, *Kindchen*?" Herr Abramowitz wanted to know.

If only I'd eaten just one grape.

Ask, Frau Abramowitz had told her, for anything you want. And she could have wanted anything. But the asking had to come first.

Maybe I can still ask—

Sick with shame, Thekla pointed to the grapes.

Frau Abramowitz lifted them. Spider stems. Her lips trembled.

"It's a difficult time for her mother right now, Ilse," Herr Abramowitz started. "You—"

"It is always a difficult time for Almut. That endless . . . needing."

"You have to understand how—"

"How often do I have to understand, Michel?" Tears on Frau Abramowitz's chin. She wiped them aside with her fingertips, but more kept coming. "Tell me. How often?"

The shame in Thekla's belly skated on the water of grapes, dizzied her. "I'm sorry." She tried her best smile, the one she could fasten on people till they smiled back.

Face wet, Frau Abramowitz tried to smile back. But only one side of her mouth went up. "Those grapes were for you, too . . . but not only for you." On the white tablecloth, her hand drifted toward Thekla, stroked her arm. "I'm sorry. I'm sorry."

"You know and I know," Herr Abramowitz said, "that this has nothing to do with grapes."

"She's like her mother. Greedy—"

"Enough. Please."

"—like her mother. And you like it, that greed in her." Frau Abramowitz raised her face. Tears on her neck, now. Tears she no longer tried to wipe away.

Tuesday, February 27, 1934

Chapter 15

HEINZ CAN SMELL HIMSELF. Camphor and dust. He was going to tell everyone about his birthday next week and the bicycle he's hoping for, but the other boys will just laugh at him. What if they can smell him, too? It's the smell of his dead grandparents' tiny house. His father says the grandparents had enough money to buy a castle, that their only joy came from spending as little as possible. All their money is hidden between the pages of books, behind pictures and furniture. Heinz is still finding banknotes—five hundred million marks, one billion marks, one hundred billion marks, one trillion marks—printed before his birth when the government kept printing new money and his father's boss paid his employees from a wheelbarrow full of banknotes that they spent quickly because in an hour it might be worthless.

His mother has told him that when she was pregnant with him, she had to pay millions for a loaf of bread. Bank accounts and bonds went *kaputt*. His parents' neighbor killed herself. His father's cousin.

But now people are beginning to hope again, his father said. Because the Führer is bringing back jobs. For everyone. Jobs and prosperity. His mother has been documenting the family's Aryan lineage for the *Ahnenpass*—ancestor report. She has told Heinz how genealogy used to be for the aristocracy only, but now it's for ordinary citizens, too. Whenever she finds out interesting details—like that her grandmother was fifteen years older than her grandfather and outlived him—she tells Heinz and his father during *Abendessen*—dinner.

Heinz's father complains it's too much effort to document every fart for the *Ahnenpass.* "But at least it'll flush out the Jews," he said. "Speaking German or going to our church does not make them Aryan."

*

"Could you please repeat what you said, Heinz?" The teacher is standing too close to him.

He wishes he were back home in the mountains, but his mother inherited the dead house, and his father is hoping to get hired at the post office, and now he must live in this flat village and go to school with mean boys.

She nods, encourages him.

"Go on," says the boy next to him. Otto.

But already Andreas is snickering from the row behind him.

When Heinz pivots, coiled fury, and hisses at him, the teacher suddenly knows what to do. *Don't single him out for not knowing. Single him out by letting him teach us.* By approaching High German as if it were a foreign language, she can motivate Heinz to translate words from his dialect into High German, which, after all, he must learn to succeed. Not just in school, but beyond. Once he can make himself understood, he won't be so awkward, and her boys will include him.

Eager to try this, she says, "We all know there are different dialects in our *Muttersprache*—mother language."

They nod, feeling smart: *We all know . . .*

"This makes our *Muttersprache* so much richer than if all of us talked the same. I don't know how many dialects we have in Germany, but I'll do some research and let you know. Any guesses?"

"Maybe twelve?" Jochen asks.

"Thirty. At least thirty," Andreas states as if saying it aloud will make it so.

"Maybe a thousand?" Eckart tries.

Several are talking at once.

The young teacher gives her boys that glance of hers—loving and disappointed—and waits as their voices spin and hum, then lessen because wanting to please her wins out. *All boys are men.*

She touches the middle groove above her lip, that short indentation. *Liebeszauber . . . Emil. No.* He'd only get in the way of her teaching position. Still—he persists in her body. *Damn.* So much for being unaffected by love. What happened to skin only? Lust only? Most days she wavers between wanting to give him up and fantasizing about going to him at night, stunning him with her passion, leaving him before dawn.

She is afraid she may be starting to love him.

—*Nein nein jetzt nicht. Weg damit*—No no not now. Away with this—

"Next week," she tells her boys, "we'll celebrate that richness of our *Muttersprache* by learning words from other dialects. Each region of our country has its own dialect, formed by history and tradition. But each region also has *Hochdeutsch*—High German, which is the German we read in books and newspapers. This means that all of you already know two languages. Most of us grew up with the dialect of the Rheinland. We're lucky to have a student who speaks the Bavarian dialect."

They all stare at Heinz, who is pulling his neck into his shoulders.

"I'll need your help with teaching us the Bavarian dialect, Heinz. Next Monday, we'll learn some words from you. You'll choose them and write them on the chalkboard, one by one, and then other students can take turns writing those word in *Hochdeutsch*."

He is embarrassed. Mumbles.

But she pretends it's agreement. "Thank you, Heinz."

Wolfgang raises his hand. "Remember, my *Opa* lives in Berlin."

"I remember."

"He has a dialect, too."

"Excellent. Next week, we'll all bring in words from other dialects. Please, find out which dialects your family knows. We'll start by learning from Heinz."

Though Heinz is watching closely, no words from him.

You should see him, Fräulein Siderova, still cautious. But I'll tutor him after school, get him to learn Hochdeutsch *by showing him my respect for his dialect. If I can teach him what he needs to know, I can protect him, make a difference in his life. Gradually, he'll be more at ease with the other boys. Thrive.*

"I'm only allowed to speak *Hochdeutsch,*" Otto says.

"My family, too," Bruno says.

"It's like that in some families," the teacher says. She wishes those two would become friends. Though Bruno comes from a better family than Otto, that can be overcome now with the new equality. What matters is that both boys are bright and thoughtful. They could learn so much from one another. She'll figure out an assignment they'll need to do together.

"My *Oma* is from the Schwarzwald," Richard says. "I know lots of words in her dialect."

"Good. You'll be second."

Heinz blinks, breathes carefully past his own smell but gets only classroom air—chalk and wool after it dries again. He wants to tell his teacher about being proud of who your ancestors were. "*Ahnenpass* . . . ," he starts, but slowly, so she can understand him.

"You're talking about documenting our ancestors," she says to him. Just to him.

Heinz nods. She *has* understood.

*

Thekla Jansen has been working on her *Ahnenpass*—ancestor report for three months now, ever since last November when Sister Mäuschen urged the faculty to have the *Ahnenpass* ready, though it's not an official requirement. Not yet. To protect the gray booklet from smudges and creases, Thekla covered it with cellophane and keeps it in her napkin holder with the documents that verify the births, weddings, and deaths of four generations.

When she read her parents' marriage certificate, she was shocked that their wedding was four months before her birth. But it wasn't like she was *unehelich*—illegitimate. Only that her parents had married sooner than planned. Many families had to rush weddings. Still, if her mother knew she'd found out, she would be mortified. That's why Thekla didn't mention it to her.

However, she had to ask about the error on her birth certificate that made her three months older than she was. "It should be January fifth, 1900," she said. "Not October fifth, 1899."

Her mother studied the certificate. "Someone must have made a mistake."

"It puts me into a different century!"

"I didn't think of it like that."

Thekla didn't speak.

"It would be easy," her mother said, "to get it reissued . . . if you'd been born here in Burgdorf. But with Nordstrand nearly six hundred kilometers away, it would take time for your request to get there. And for them to send you the corrected birth certificate."

"I want to be done with this." All Thekla was waiting for were two more originals, the wedding certificate of her parents and the birth certificate of her paternal great-grandmother. Once they arrived, she'd complete her *Ahnenpass* and take it to the town hall for seals and signatures.

"Remember how slow they were in Nordstrand, getting you the death certificates of your father's brother and sisters?"

Thekla shivered. "Those dead children . . . birth dates spread over four years but their day of death the same."

"When we lived on Nordstrand, I often walked with your *Oma* by the sea at dawn."

"What if I just used the date that's already on my birth certificate?"

Mutti didn't answer. So many freckles on her cheeks that she looked sun-brown in winter. Raising one hand, she touched Thekla's chin. "Sometimes I want to tell you . . ."

"Tell me what?"

Mutti dropped her hand. Tugged it beneath her apron. "Maybe you can give your students the assignment to search their family trees. How many of them can recite the names of their eight great-grandparents?"

"I don't know."

"Your father, he knew the names of his great-grandparents."

Your father . . . Thekla wondered how much her students knew about her father. Some probably had never seen him because he'd barely been outdoors in years. But people talked. Maybe some parents said, "Your teacher's father, he is crazy."

"He used to be interested in genealogy," Thekla's mother continued, "but once he came back from the war, his mind was . . . broken."

Moments like this Thekla felt the legacy of his craziness waiting for her, though she told herself that he hadn't been born with it, that it had first come into him when the wave took his siblings, and that it hadn't caught him fully till the Great War.

Chapter 16

"TO RECITE SOMETHING," she tells her boys, "will plant it inside your mind: poetry, multiplication, history dates."

That's how Fräulein Siderova taught when Thekla was her student, and when they sang Heinrich Heine's "Loreley," the girls could feel the sadness the poet described, haunting him over a fairy tale from ancient times:

Ich weiss nicht, was soll es bedeuten,
dass ich so traurig bin;
ein Märchen aus alten Zeiten,
das geht mir nicht aus dem Sinn.

Fräulein Siderova told them that more than twenty composers had set Heine's poem to music. But long before Heine, Brentano and Keats had already written about the enchantress who—from a cliff in the Rhein near St. Goarshausen—lured sailors to crash their ships on the rocks.

*

Thekla feels frustrated that Heine's poems are now forbidden. If only she could teach them to her boys, they'd recognize his descriptions of their Rhein, of the sun at dusk. She'd tell them how he grew up near Burgdorf more than a hundred years ago, and she'd lead them into writing descriptions of their village and let them discover—within their own words—how poetry was possible for every one of them.

With Heine they would identify, much more so than last week with old Walther von der Vogelweide, one of the earliest poets listed in the Echtermeyer, who did his writing more than seven centuries ago, too early to offend this government. When Thekla assigned her boys an essay based on his work, she gave it the title "My Daily Life Seven Hundred Years Ago," and encouraged the boys to be precise in what they imagined.

A lot of her favorite writers are now on the list of un-German writers: Bertolt Brecht and Anna Seghers and Franz Werfel and Erich Kästner . . .

All of Heine's books are banned, not only because he was Jewish but because some of his poems criticized Germany. *You can think those things but not say them aloud. Or, worse yet, write them down for everyone to read.* That's why she taught her boys Brentano's version of the Loreley legend. They were excited about the gold of the Nibelungen, hidden deep in the Rhein below Loreley's cliff. Rhein maidens watched over it, but Alberich stole the gold and forced the Nibelungen tribe to forge it into a ring that would give him power over the world. Gold and caves and dragons fascinated her boys. Something disguised as a treasure even more so.

Some say that Heinrich Heine dirtied his nest and then moved away, to Paris, where he wrote another poem about being unable to sleep when he thinks of Germany at night:

Denk ich an Deutschland in der Nacht,
Dann bin ich um den Schlaf gebracht . . .

Heinrich Heine, cursing the false *Vaterland* where only dishonor and disgrace flourished. Jeopardizing himself and—beyond his death—anyone who reads his poems, or wants to teach them.

*

Thekla dreads her conversation with the Stosicks tonight. They'll probably blame her for encouraging Bruno when he joined the Hitler-Jugend. Of course she knows the Nazis are crass and common. But she also knows they're temporary, and that she can wait them out. She can't say this to Bruno's parents. They're so critical of the Führer that they may quote her. Don't they see that nothing will ever totally match their ideals? Why not use what they can for their son?

Bruno wants to belong, to win awards. For his sake, she must find one thing she and his parents can agree on. Maybe she'll emphasize the Hitler-Jugend as a stepping-stone to the best secondary schools and apprenticeships. "Everything is just for now," she'll say, "and if we keep waiting for something we totally approve of, we'll miss the next stepping-stone."

But she'll have to be diplomatic: Günther Stosick is a principal; she only a first-year teacher. She'll remind him of the shame that used to fill the space where pride once lived, and how—as teachers—they have a responsibility to restore that pride in their students. "Knowledge without pride is fragile," she may say.

"We were more human without it."

She's getting agitated just thinking of what he may say. But all at once she feels relieved. Because it's Tuesday. And that means she can't speak with them tonight.

*

Every Tuesday the members of the Burgdorf Chess Club meet in the Stosicks' living room: they get out the chess sets and chess clocks and books from the birch wardrobe, set up four long tables, and cover them with starched white tablecloths. Usually, they play past midnight.

So far, Bruno has won against every man, including brilliant strategists like his father and Leo Montag. The boy plays without effort, it seems to the members, though that is of course unthinkable because what would that say about their game?

A boy like that can make you fear that at fifty-one, say, or forty-three, you are too old to learn more about chess.

A boy like that can make you wish you'd spoken out against allowing children in the club.

Already, Bruno is competing on a national level, and it's obvious that, in a few years, he'll bring honor to his chess club and all of Burgdorf by representing Germany in international tournaments.

A few weeks ago his father showed Thekla the first chess ledgers, dating back to the beginning of the nineteenth century and documenting every game by the members of the club. "These early entries are in the handwriting of the founder," he said with reverence.

Gisela rolled her eyes.

"Must you?" he asked, but he seemed amused.

"Obviously, the members, including my dear husband, worship this idiot of a founder. And you know why? Because that man abandoned his eight children and his wife for the greatest passion of all . . . chess." As Gisela drew out the word *chess* into several syllables, she looked about ten years old.

At ten, Gisela had been impish and swift at the piano, and she'd become the protégée of Frau Birnsteig, the concert pianist, who still invited the townspeople to her mansion every June to hear her play the piano for them—Debussy and Beethoven and Rachmaninoff—and to introduce her current protégée to this audience.

*

Better talk to the Stosicks tomorrow morning. She'll wait till she hears the first steps downstairs, quick and light: Gisela. Maybe it would be best to speak with her alone, let her persuade Günther. Yes, Thekla decides, she'll stay upstairs till she hears the front door, wait by her window till she sees the top of Günther Stosick's hat, the herringbone pattern of his coat, as he heads in the direction of the Protestant school.

Then she'll go down to the kitchen, where Gisela keeps her piano in the breakfast nook, windows on three sides. It's the only place for it since the living room is for chess. But Gisela likes to play her piano here. She'll ask Thekla to sit at her table, offer her coffee. Her hair will be sticking up, the way it gets from sleeping without a pillow.

On excursions with their youth group, Gisela would wake up with her hair stiff like that. Maybe they can talk about roasting potatoes in the fire, poking at them as they turned black with the embers. With the sharpened ends of bare branches, they'd impale the crisp skins to the soft centers and raise the potatoes, slowly, so they wouldn't drop back into the flames. They'd blow on them, impatient to bite through the skins into the white insides. Black around their mouths, then, and they'd become the beast, scare one another by stretching their smudged lips and howling.

"Not all that different from what the children do now . . . hikes and songs and stories," Thekla will say.

"I loved to stare into the flames," Gisela may say.

"But one night you disappeared."

Gisela will shake her head, smile. "Do you have to remind me of that?"

"When we couldn't find you, the group leaders divided us into groups of five. We were forbidden to separate while we searched and yelled your name."

"I never heard you shout."

"We thought you'd been kidnapped. Raped. Killed."

"Too many stories around the fire . . ."

"Instead you were asleep on that platform," Thekla will say, prompting Gisela to tell her part of the adventure again: how she had climbed up the rungs of the ladder to that observation platform where, the day before, the girls had taken a picnic of cheese *Brötchen* and apples and lemonade.

"But why climb up there middle of the night?" Thekla will ask. "You were scared of being alone."

Quite likely, Gisela will say she doesn't remember. It's what she has said before.

But Thekla won't believe her because she, too, has not forgotten the wide-swirling path of light in the sky that spanned north and south, weightless and imposing.

Chapter 17

RAIN AGAINST THE windows of the schoolhouse. Hard.

"Close your eyes, boys," Fräulein Jansen says, "and listen to the rain. Imagine rain on the grasses and the fields. . . ."

Some press their lids shut, twitchy folds.

Others let their lids slide down, smooth orbs.

"Think of the impossible green of wet treetops. . . ."

They raise their faces toward her, blind, expectant.

I wish you could see them, Fräulein Siderova.

"Listen closely: *pluie.*"

"Pluie?" asks Walter.

"Yes, *pluie.* The French word for rain. It's also what rain sounds like, doesn't it?"

"Pluie . . . ," whispers Otto. He bets Markus knows the word. Markus had private lessons in French. And in art. Otto misses planning with him about how the two of them would learn the

entire knowledge of the entire world and store it inside their minds: all languages, all art, all history. They'd go to university together, become teachers like Fräulein Jansen.

"Keep your eyes closed and listen. . . ." The teacher is listening to the rain, too, thinking how it was raining this hard seven weeks ago.

She remembers because of Marinus van der Lubbe. The Dutch queen, Wilhelmina Helena Pauline Maria, had appealed on his behalf to the old President von Hindenburg, asking him to commute her subject's sentence to prison because at the time of his arrest the penalty for arson was not death—not yet. At dawn, on January 10, while the queen was still waiting for the answer to her appeal, the young Dutchman was taken from his solitary cell. Through the wet grass of the Leipzig prison yard, the executioner—white gloves, top hat—led Marinus to the guillotine.

At exactly twenty-eight minutes and fifty-five seconds past the hour of seven, his head dropped into a basket of sawdust.

Three days later, Marinus would have turned twenty-five.

Nearly seventy-five years later his verdict, guilty, would be revoked by the German federal prosecutor.

*

Sometimes, at dawn, Marinus inserts himself into the young teacher's sleep-awareness. Like this morning, when she was still adrift in half-sleep, and the gentle weight of her feather quilt felt like that of a lover bending over her. *Emil?* But as she burrowed deeper into her bedding, the one with her was the Dutchman Marinus without the buttoned jacket he wore in newspaper photos, moon on his chest. The first night in her apartment she had dragged the bed to the window though it would block her way to the door, but she wanted the moon on her pillow, on her throat, her breasts. And in this moon, *now,* the mouth of the young Dutchman, sullen. His eyes no longer clown's eyes because the shadow of his cap is gone.

Yet his black hair still in the shape of that cap, straight up from his forehead. *Marinus. Hands fast, hands gentle—*

Thekla's left foot slid across the sheet where her mother had darned it with embroidery thread that she split into single strands, her stitches so delicate you could find them only by touch, a silkier weave than the surrounding linen. *Don't think—*

Hands fast, hands gentle on her breasts her belly her thighs her buttocks—hands with rough skin, hands of a bricklayer—

How would Marinus's life have gone if someone had taken him to Russia? "Here, this is where you want to be. So be here." But before he could leave Holland, he'd had an accident. Five months in the hospital and an invalid's pension. Enough to make it to Germany, but not to Russia.

Not yet, no, she was almost there, almost, hands of a bricklayer—

But the hands were her own, not rough, and Marinus's head was cut off forever—

*

Struck by sorrow for him, Thekla sat up. Pulled the quilt around her shoulders. Through the open door, she could see the kitchen table and her napkin holder with her gray *Ahnenpass* booklet and the supporting documentation of her ancestors. Next to it were two stacks of clothes and linens, ironed and folded. *Mutti* must have been here yesterday evening while Thekla was out dancing with Emil. She had a key, always let herself in to pick up laundry and return it, clean. *Mutti* says Thekla is good at nesting. And that's true. Thekla likes making a home with a few belongings that matter to her: a pottery jar with dried cornflowers; the basket where she stores gifts she's bought for Fräulein Siderova: a blue glass egg, a beveled glass box for jewelry, a glass figure of a ballerina that would remind Fräulein Siderova of taking ballet lessons as a girl in Russia.

At least once a week *Mutti* stayed for a long bath. Thekla's cylinder stove could heat more water than even her mother could want.

In the tub, she would hum to herself, turn the faucet with her toes to add more hot water whenever she wanted, gray-blond tendrils on her cheeks and shoulders. For so many years, she'd taken shallow baths in the basin she'd fill once a week in her kitchen with water she'd heat in all her pots. She'd tack a bedsheet across the kitchen and sponge herself clean behind that, humming, singing. The children would get to bathe in the water afterward. Then *Vati*. It was the only place where *Mutti* insisted on being first.

Thekla snaked one hand from the warmth of her bed to get a cigarette from her nightstand. Only then did she bring out her other hand and tap the cigarette against her wrist. The hiss of sulfur, then the familiar ease, that first blue drag through her body . . . *ja* . . . before she curled it down her throat, practiced, the smoke of her cigarette a shade duller than the frost on her window.

*

"Fräulein?"

She coughs, embarrassed.

"Pluie . . ."

"Can we open our eyes?"

"If you like," she says. "But keep thinking of raindrops striking a puddle, or a pail . . . causing rings to form before they bounce off the surface, but not as high as where they come from."

Her boys are nodding.

". . . *Pluie,"* Andreas says.

"Pluie . . . Very good. Glistening rain, washing the roofs, the leaves . . . and a world within each raindrop— Would you like to know what the Italians call rain?" she asks.

"Ja."

"Pioggia."

"Pioggia," her boys call out.

1904–1907

Chapter 18

IT WAS RAINING like that the afternoon Frau Abramowitz hoisted Thekla onto her desk in the living room and told her the most beautiful word in all languages was *rain*. "*Pioggia* in Italian. Now you say it."

Thekla moved her lips around the Italian word like Frau Abramowitz did, heard the sound of herself saying, *"Pioggia,"* and the sounds of pots and dishes from the kitchen, where her mother was washing the dishes.

"That's excellent," Frau Abramowitz said. "Try it again, a bit softer. *Pioggia.*"

"Pioggia?"

"Very good. Now in French: *pluie.*"

Above the desk hung the little mirror Frau Abramowitz had bought in Venice, shiny with gold around it

"Pluie . . . pluie—" Thekla tilted her head. "Like rain . . . on the roof."

"Such a brilliant little girl." Frau Abramowitz smiled at her. Fine wrinkles, so many that her skin looked all of one piece, not one wrinkle standing out.

"Thekla," *Mutti* called.

Frau Abramowitz jerked her head aside.

Empty. Thekla's hand empty now. *Something wrong, I've done something wrong—what is it?—and the shame of that.*

Quickly, Frau Abramowitz lifted Thekla from her desk. "Go to your mother now."

—greedy like her mother—grapes, stolen grapes like water, green and cool and light—

—Nein nein jetzt nicht. Weg damit—No no not now. Away with this—

—and already no longer remembering but knowing it can come back—

Frau Abramowitz flung open the glass doors to her garden. In the cold rain she picked violets. *Mutti* rinsed a crystal vase and filled it with water for her. After Frau Abramowitz arranged the violets in the vase, she set it on top of her piano and fussed with her little picture frames. The oldest photo was of her husband's mother, Judith, as an infant in a wicker carriage outside the arched front door of this house.

*

It was that very photo Judith Abramowitz had kept by her bedside during the final months of her life—not pictures of her husband and children, only this one of herself—because in that final paring down her most enduring link was to herself. Instead of wearing the quilted bed jacket her daughter-in-law, Ilse, had bought for her, Judith Abramowitz asked for her silk piano shawl with the white fringes, and she draped it around her shoulders and breasts and arms.

During the past year she'd given thought to choosing the most beautiful piece of glass she could find, hoping its beauty would ensure the beauty of her death once Fräulein Siderova arrived to read poems to her in her final hours. When that day came, Sonja Siderova could see that Judith Abramowitz was afraid of encountering her *Vater* after death. Still, she kept reading, and in her voice, Judith recognized the wisdom of one who had crossed countless times, one who could guide her, too, on that passage until she was ready to continue on her own. She yielded, let the fear be until it let her be, until she saw how it had all passed in one blink, from the baby in the wicker carriage to this old woman who—although motionless in the shimmer of folds and fringes of the shawl—felt herself moving with startling grace.

*

Three nights and three days the rain came in torrents, silver and steady, too steady for Thekla to go outdoors and find a treasure for her *Vati*. So she searched indoors. On the second day of rain, she brought him *Mutti*'s rosary. As she tugged the wooden beads, one by one, through his slack fingers, it came to her that his hands were like the carvings of an apprentice toymaker, not of the master toymaker he was. It wasn't right. She yanked at the beads, a flicker of prayers that would shorten his stay in purgatory and give him a soft chair in heaven.

On the third day of rain, she brought *Vati* a photo from inside the lining of *Mutti*'s sewing basket. Thekla was good at finding things—too good, *Mutti* liked to say—because whenever something was hidden, it would tug at Thekla's mind till she had to go find it.

She laid the picture into *Vati*'s hands. It was of Frau Abramowitz holding a baby, both floating in the air. But the photo was all blurry from Frau Abramowitz's tears. Why was she crying? Why—

Behind her a sharp breath. *Mutti.* Who snatched the photo away.

But *Vati* was still staring at his palms where the photo had been just a moment ago.

Thekla's curls felt heavy from the damp air.

"Where did you get this?" *Mutti* cried and hid the photo under her apron. "Don't you go snooping for this again."

That's why Thekla had to get a new picture for *Vati.*

She drew it for him. Of Noah's Ark. Two of each kind to save during the flood. The animals were easy. And so was choosing the woman: *Mutti.* But then for the man? Herr Abramowitz or *Vati*? Thekla's throat hurt from thinking. She'd seen the Rhein flow into her street. Had heard stories of other floods that had come inside houses and drowned people and carried away what belonged to them. If she took *Vati* on the ark, he'd sit in the middle of it, hands dropping from his bony wrists like dead things. But Herr Abramowitz was strong and fast. He could build the world all over again.

Mutti covered her mouth when Thekla showed her the drawing. "Don't let *Vati see.*"

"But I'm taking you on the ark . . . and Herr Abramowitz—"

"Your *Vati* would be sad."

"—and a girl and a boy and giraffes and cows and bees."

*

Her mother must have shown Herr Abramowitz the drawing, because he sent the paperhanger, who pasted yellow wallpaper on the walls of Thekla's bedroom and, along the top, a water-blue border of Noah's Ark. All around her room: the ark and Noah and his wife and two of each kind of child and two of each animal, all in a row till it came to the ark again and the people and the animals.

Now that the flood was in Thekla's room, it felt urgent that she choose who was to be on her ark. But soon, mold bloomed from the lower edge of the border, a sign that the flood was receding. Now she wouldn't have to leave *Vati* behind. She was relieved.

But Herr Abramowitz said the paperhanger must have done something wrong and made him come back to remove the border. Thekla screamed and stomped till *Mutti* took her by the wrists and pulled her outside.

"I have to save *Vati* from drowning."

Mutti's lips trembled. "What did he tell you?"

"The flood—"

"None of us will drown." *Mutti* lifted her into her arms.

After *Mutti* sent the paperhanger away, she filled a pail with water and soap, climbed on a chair, and scrubbed the mold away. But Thekla was glad when it grew back in lush shadings of gray, lit by green and yellow, purple even.

Chapter 19

EVEN AFTER Michel Abramowitz would have children with his wife, Ilse, he would never attach to them with this all-consuming love he felt for his firstborn, Thekla, a love that carried as much bereavement as bliss. And yet, there was the relief at the convenience of not having to be near her all the time, and the delight he could bring his daughter when he'd step inside her kitchen as if he lived right outside her front door. While Michel filled the house with food and with his deep laugh, the toymaker would retreat into the cave of his body.

Ilse argued that it caused talk where talk could be avoided, but he wanted to provide for his child, and Almut encouraged that, though she did not encourage him in other ways. She'd thank him, politely. Always, now, polite and aloof with him, as if all he'd ever been to her was her employer, as if she wanted him to believe he had only imagined her mouth *verführerisch*—seductive.

Of course the townspeople speculated that he was Thekla's *Vater*. It was easy to figure out why Almut Jansen kept working for his family: jobs were scarce, and she was treated better than most domestics. But why did Ilse Abramowitz tolerate her? Granted, Almut's darning was exquisite, her ironing flawless, but that hardly outweighed having her in the house six days a week. How did Ilse Abramowitz tolerate Almut Jansen's hands on the clothes she wore next to her skin . . . washing, sewing, folding? Her husband's clothes, too. Perhaps, some reasoned, Ilse kept her on because Michel wouldn't let her dismiss Almut. But those who knew Ilse well said she was too smart for ultimatums. More likely, she'd made a trade with her husband: Almut could work in their house as long as he kept away from her.

*

Thekla liked to hold the pail with wooden clothespins while *Mutti* lifted the damp laundry from the basket. The freckles on *Mutti*'s arms didn't reach the undersides, puffy and white. She could wring out more water than anyone else. Each piece of clothing she'd snap into the wind and, in its billowing, fasten that shape to the washline by a hem, say, or the ends of sleeves. Though she washed everything with Henkel's Persil, the Abramowitzes' laundry was brighter than the Jansens' and claimed more space on the line, while the Jansens' shirts and nightgowns were bunched at the far ends.

Every morning Thekla went with her to the Abramowitzes' house. It stood tall across the street from the pay-library, grocery store, and tailor shop. Whenever *Mutti* carried the basket with the Abramowitzes' ironed laundry, Thekla would hold on to its edge, from Hindenburg Strasse to Schreberstrasse, through the Abramowitzes' arched door, into airy rooms that were bright even on cloudy days, and up the stairs to the big bedroom.

One afternoon, when *Mutti* knelt by the dressing table to arrange the clean laundry inside, Thekla scooted around her and sat on *Mutti*'s bent knees, felt the hard belly behind her. Baby-belly from the stork. Storks lived on the highest rooftops.

In the mirror, *Mutti* kissed the top of Thekla's hair. "That woman always wants what's mine," she whispered and glanced toward the open door. "She'd love to keep you here without me. But she knows I'll take you with me wherever I go." When she tossed her head, one of her hairpins slipped from her coiled braid.

Thekla picked it up.

"Always after me, 'Do this and do that right now. . . .'"

Thekla was puzzled. At home *Mutti* was the one to say, "Do this and do that." And Thekla obeyed. But in this house Frau Abramowitz said to *Mutti,* "Do this and do that." And *Mutti* obeyed.

In church everyone obeyed the priest. On the church steps, too.

*

After mass, last Sunday, Thekla had found a feather in the puddle by the church steps where *Mutti* stood with Herr Pastor Schüler.

"If you keep praying, God will hear you," he said to her. His body was little, but his voice was so big it could save your soul.

The old pharmacist edged closer. "Excellent sermon, Herr Pastor Schüler." His voice was the best in the choir, melodious and steady.

"Thank you." The priest beamed and scratched his chest through his vestment. Powder drifted from beneath, settled on his shoes and on the ground by the edge of the puddle.

Mutti stepped aside.

"I'm still waiting for your husband's medicine," the pharmacist said to her.

"He has enough for a week."

"Good. I'll send the delivery boy once it gets here."

"Thank you." *Mutti* reached for Thekla's hand. As soon as they were out of the church square, she whispered, "Those priests, they lie."

Thekla's feather was still wet when she lifted *Vati*'s hands and curved his fingers till they had to close around the feather. The rim of his white shirt was frayed but clean between his hairy-blond wrists and the black sleeves of his good suit. His left thumb twitched as it tested the fine strands. *Falling then, Wilhelm, falling . . . and getting smaller and water in his mouth . . . forever falling—*

*

Mutti pulled her other hairpins from her braid, turning it into crinkly angel hair. She pushed it from her cheeks, studied her face in the mirror of the dressing table. "That woman already has wrinkles. Her mother had skin like that."

Thekla stretched herself tall until her brown hair was below *Mutti*'s chin. Laughing, *Mutti* shook her angel hair, let it ripple around Thekla's face, and touched the ends of her hair below Thekla's nose in a blond mustache. Thekla giggled, leaned against *Mutti*'s apron, soft from countless washings. The baby-belly squirmed.

Suddenly three heads in the mirror—

Brown, blond, brown.

Frau Abramowitz's head above *Mutti*'s, Thekla's below.

Till *Mutti* stood up and was the same as Frau Abramowitz. In height. But not in clothing because Frau Abramowitz's belly—big like *Mutti*'s belly, big from the stork—was under her silk dress as if her baby were already wearing silk. In that awkward silence, Thekla could feel the inequality, and though she didn't yet have the word to define it, she would recognize it from now on, separating the rich and their servants, from whom they expected compliance, gratitude.

Frau Abramowitz did not open her arms for Thekla the way she did when she was alone with her. She had such a sad face that Thekla made herself smile at her—she was good at making others smile back—but Frau Abramowitz didn't.

Mutti bent to kiss Thekla's ear, whispered, "That woman's smile muscles are broken."

So that's what it was. Except it wasn't. Confusing. Because sometimes Frau Abramowitz smiled at Thekla. Like when she was alone with her. Or when she read to her. Or when she taught her how to count in the foreign languages she knew from her travels and told her she was a natural striver.

Mutti reached up to braid her hair, and as she wound it into a coil, her arms were like the arms of two different mothers, freckled on top but pale underneath. Thekla waited for the freckles to slide so that *Mutti*'s skin would be all the same color.

*

Thekla's brother Elmar was born the following week, Ruth Abramowitz five weeks later. Thekla felt grown-up because she was the helper now.

When Frau Abramowitz saw Elmar in his wicker carriage outside the pay-library, she kissed his forehead, stroked his chin. "What a beautiful boy," she said.

"Thank you," *Mutti* said.

"Blond like your husband."

Mutti blinked. Tightened her hands on the handle of the wicker carriage. Walked with it so quickly that Thekla had to run next to her. "I have to make this work," she whispered. "I have to . . ."

At home, she sat down and, without taking off her shoes, propped her feet on the brocade ottoman Frau Abramowitz had given her.

*

Soon both mothers had baby-bellies again, and Dietrich Jansen was born in July 1905, Albert Abramowitz in August. Thekla didn't understand why her little brothers had to stay with Frau Brocker across the street while she got to accompany *Mutti* to the tall house, where Frau Abramowitz read to her and took her to the playground.

She missed her brothers. When she asked *Mutti* why they couldn't come along, *Mutti* said, "It's because you're special."

But it didn't feel right to Thekla that she had the big corner bedroom to herself, lace and curtains and sun, while Elmar and

Dietrich shared a bed in the cubby off the kitchen, where they moved like flashes of sun as they climbed up and down the shelves that used to be for storage. Here, they played with each other. Only with each other. With Thekla they were watchful.

*

Early morning, and Elmar was crying, fussing when they arrived in Frau Brocker's kitchen.

He held on to *Mutti*'s waist. "I go with you."

She bit her lip. Shook her head.

"I go with—"

"Come, now," Frau Brocker said to him.

But he refused to let go of his *Mutti*. "Why not?" he sobbed.

"Because . . ." Gently, Frau Brocker pulled him away, lifted him into her wide arm, and kissed the tears on his cheeks. "Because Frau Abramowitz likes girls. Isn't that silly?"

He squinted at Thekla, hatred in his eyes.

She winced. Offered quickly, "I'll ask Frau Abramowitz."

"You won't do any such thing," *Mutti* said. "You're lucky I can bring you."

"Lucky . . . ," Elmar chanted and clapped his hands. "Lucky . . ."

*

Thekla brought *Vati* a dead mouse because she wanted him to feel the difference between the velvety belly and the harsh fur. She pried his fingers apart, set the mouse into his palms, took his thumb and rubbed it across the mouse. Tried to close his hand around it. And gradually, his fingers quivered. Found the difference.

"Don't you put dead things into *Vati's* hands." Elmar pushed her away. "You're like a cat. Carrying dead mice." Big ears and pale stick-up hair. A prissy boy who would grow into a crude man. Who could not see that she was bringing *Vati* treasures.

This mouse.

Or a few grains of soil.

Soil that was different from soil in another area.

Grasses.

A thistle.

Opening *Vati* up. Teaching him through touch.

But Elmar yelled at her. "Touching dead things! You'll turn blue."

"And then you die," Dietrich said.

There was nothing that felt like the belly of a mouse. *Vati* understood.

Frau Abramowitz would understand, too. She would say, "What a good teacher you are, Thekla."

But Elmar said, "Wash your hands, Thekla."

Tuesday, February 27, 1934

Chapter 20

"IMAGINE FORTY DAYS of rain," Thekla says to her students. "That's what Noah and his family had."

"That's why he built the ark," Eckart says.

"That's true. Now if we had forty days of rain, what would you bring along?"

Her boys don't even mention what-to-bring, go right into whom-to-bring. Or rather, whom-not-to-bring.

"If we take everyone, we'll sink," says Walter.

Andreas Beil nods. "The Führer won't let any Jews on the ark."

Thekla feels queasy. *This's not what I mean.* This morning when she arrived at school, Sister Mäuschen, timid and gray-skinned, was scurrying past the St. Christopher statue at the far end of the corridor. *Mäuschen. Little Mouse.* So shy and fast and little, it might vanish if you came too close. As she did this morning, vanish, just as Thekla got close enough to see that she'd put up a poster for a film on *Rassenreinheit*—racial purity, one of those wretched films that claimed Jews were filthy in their moral and physical habits. Infuriating, having to watch another film like this. Humiliating, having to hold back what you really thought.

Several boys are talking about a flag with a swastika for their ark.

"Actually," the teacher explains, "the swastika is an ancient symbol that means sun and life and luck . . . and power."

"How ancient?" Franz wants to know.

"At least three thousand years. It was used by different races. In India and in China and in Troy and—"

Andreas shakes his head. "It's just for the Aryan race. That's what the Führer says."

She reminds herself that she can reach the most difficult students, that with every one of them there's a different way of opening up. "On our next visit to the museum in Düsseldorf, we'll research the swastika," she tells Andreas. "We'll start with some coins and pottery from Greece that have the swastika on them."

*

Otto raises his hand. "With all the animals on the ark, there should be frogs, too."

"Absolutely." She walks to the piano, leans across the frog house to watch Icarus.

Otto nudges Heinz. "We can take Icarus."

"Icarus," Heinz says. "Yes."

It strikes the teacher that Otto seems more grown-up than the other boys, more of a man already. That's probably why they sometimes look to him for direction.

"But Icarus doesn't need the ark," Eckart says. "He can swim."

"Yes," Otto says, "but we need him."

"Why?"

"Remember, two of each animal on the ark," Otto says. "Besides, Icarus has become weak. And a flood is not the time to release him."

The boys have talked about setting Icarus free in the moat that encircles the Sternburg, in the same spot where they found him, under the drawbridge. They've talked about having waited too long. But they want to believe that, come summer, Icarus will be stronger again; his tongue will once again dart for the flies that taunt him by standing still in the air, wings humming until, with a sudden jolt, they'll dodge Icarus just as he is about to leap and snatch them.

"From the day we caught him," the teacher says, "we've planned to release him. But in the meantime we've learned about the risk of removing an animal from its habitat." She motions for her boys to come close. "How do we weigh that then—the risk to him versus the learning it brings us?"

As the boys crowd around the glass house, Icarus squeezes himself between two cushions of moss.

"But we didn't know about the risk," Richard says.

"Not when we caught Icarus," Walter adds.

She nods. Waits.

"But what if finding that out is part of learning, too?" Eckart asks.

"More flies," Heinz says quietly.

"Yes," Otto says, "we can feed Icarus more flies. Maybe then it is not too late for him."

Andreas says, "I found a sack with new—"

But Richard interrupts him. "When can we release Icarus?"

"Come spring we will." The teacher sits down at the piano and plays the first melody that comes to her, Schumann's rendition of Eichendorff's poem, *"Der Frohe Wandersmann"*—"The Happy Wanderer." It's one her boys learned from her, and they sing with her about the rivers and forests, larks and wind. Fräulein Siderova liked to say that, if you sang a poem, it planted itself inside you twice, so that you could recall it through melody and words.

*

"Roller skates." Andreas's voice is hopping with excitement. "The unknown benefactor left them for me. In a sack. On my front stoop."

Suddenly her boys are talking all at once.

"The unknown benefactor left a big block of cheese in our kitchen," Otto says.

" . . . a bicycle for my father," Eckart is saying.

"Your manners," the young teacher reminds them.

Bruno and Markus come from good families, but most of her boys she has to remind of their manners. You can absorb refinement only as a child. The Führer talks about bringing out the best in the youth of Germany, but he'll never have that for himself. He may have learned how to thank others properly, how to eat with his fork in his left hand and his knife in his right, but it's obvious he learned this as an adult.

Her boys nudge each other to be quiet, to wait for her to call on them.

She adjusts her scarf. Children like strong colors, and she always wears something bright for them, her yellow-and-blue scarf, say, or her green blouse. She enjoys dressing up for her boys, enjoys it when their mothers tell her the wildness in their sons has settled into thoughtfulness ever since she became their teacher.

"Yes, Franz?" she says.

"The unknown benefactor brought us three new blankets."

Every few months, the Burgdorf *Post* runs another article about the unknown benefactor, whose identity is still a mystery despite two decades of gifts on people's doorsteps or inside their homes. People agree it has to be someone from Burgdorf because these gifts are always what you need or hope for: coats and shoes in the proper sizes, a phonograph and records, medicine and food. And now roller skates for Andreas Beil, who will indeed become a policeman and—nine years from now—find himself devastated when it's discovered that the vandal he's shot for dismantling a Hitler monument, crusted with pigeon shit, has been the benefactor all along. Only in death will the identity become known.

Chapter 21

CAN I BRING my roller skates to school after lunch?" Andreas asks his teacher.

"Soon," she tells him. "Once the sidewalks are clear again."

She motions to Jochen Weskopp to present his butterfly collection to the class, and he unwraps three kitchen towels, holds up a frame with green felt backing, and explains about catching and mounting butterflies.

Last week Andreas brought a dozen pictures he'd drawn of policemen. The week before Bruno demonstrated chess moves on the rosewood chess set he'd inherited from his grandfather. Not quite what Sister Josefine envisioned when she suggested teachers ask their students to bring in items that related to the Great War. Thekla doesn't rule out that one or two, indeed, may choose something a father or uncle stashed away from his days as a soldier, but it's too soon to introduce these children to war.

It's far more valuable for them to bring in items that matter to them, that excite them so much they want to tell the class about them. That's how each boy learns from himself. That's how they learn about one another. Thekla loves it when she can anchor knowledge inside them through their passions, instead of fighting their discouragement that they are ignorant, or that it's hard to learn something new.

When she thanks Jochen, he's pleased. Since Lent is on the curriculum, she'll fit it in now, before today's faculty meeting, so that—while her boys go home to eat lunch and recover from theories of sacrifice—she can report to her colleagues that she's already taught Lent. Too many meetings. Evening meetings, too. But as a teacher you are a government employee, and it is wise to join the party, to be seen. Some parents have complained that their children don't have enough time for play and being with their families.

Most of her colleagues can't separate propaganda from truth, but Thekla knows the difference, knows that being true to yourself doesn't necessarily mean you are truthful, knows how to use reverence—a hand to her throat, a deep sigh—during meetings to prove her loyalty. After all, she has felt that reverence as a child in church, the emotional pitch that proves your transformation. Easy enough to use that reverence in politics.

*

"Now, we still have our lesson on Lent," she says.

Walter has his hand up.

"Yes, Walter?"

"Jesus started Lent."

She nods. "He fasted in the desert for forty days in preparation for his death and resurrection. That's why the church asks us to give up things we like for Lent."

"Forty days and forty nights he fasted," Walter reminds her. "That's why we fast and take inventory of our sins."

"Thank you."

"In my family we give up second helpings for Lent," says Wolfgang. Of course. One of the few families where second helpings are available. Because of his uncle's barbershop.

"No applesauce yesterday," Otto says.

Other boys report what they are giving up.

"No meat."

"I only eat one egg a week, not two."

"Marmalade."

Thekla remembers a praline Frau Abramowitz slipped into her hand one Lent when she was four or five. Gold foil wrap. Inside nougat and chocolate with half a walnut on top. When Thekla said it was Lent, Frau Abramowitz said, "Don't wait to live," and folded Thekla's fingers across the praline.

"If you break Lent, you get a tapeworm," Andreas says.

"That is not true," Richard says.

"It's a superstition," the teacher says.

Andreas shakes his head. "But it's what my father says."

"Another way of approaching Lent," she says, "is that you don't have to give up anything."

Some frown at her; others lean forward.

"Instead you are learning how to wait for what you want, and that's a good skill to have. Just remind yourself that you can have everything—only not right away. And that you'll enjoy it more on Easter Sunday because you've waited for it."

"Why is Easter on a different date every year?" Richard asks.

"It has to do with the moon. Easter is on the first Sunday after the first full moon after March twenty-first. Yes, Otto?"

"So the people who make the calendar start with Easter? And then they count back forty days to the first day of Lent?"

"Yes, and that's *Aschermittwoch*—Ash Wednesday."

"This year *Aschermittwoch* was early," Eckart says. "That's why Easter will be early, too."

"And Palm Sunday, when Jesus made his triumphant entry into Jerusalem," Walter says, excited to be talking about Jesus. "After Palm Sunday, the priests burn the palms and store the ashes for tracing the cross on our foreheads."

*

"Next week," the teacher says, "each of you will write an essay about the life of his namesake saint. When you research your saints, ask questions. Don't expect to find out everything at once. Ask your parents, the priest, the sisters. Take notes. Especially if you think you already know, ask." It's what Herr Abramowitz used to tell her. "I learned that from a . . . family friend," she adds. "An educated man who always encouraged me to ask questions."

She gathers her notes, stops to salute when her students leave, a rush toward the door, toward home where their mothers or grandmothers are waiting for them with lunch.

Sobbing—

It makes her think of her little brother, sobbing before his first communion, terrified of touching the wafer with his teeth. "It's a sin if you chew it. Herr Pastor Schüler said never ever let your teeth touch it."

And she, calming Dietrich. "When he puts it on your tongue, you pull it in without letting it touch your teeth."

"But I'll choke."

"Just push it with your tongue to the roof of your mouth." Showing him. Opening her mouth wide and wiggling her tongue. "Like this. Afterward you swallow it a bit at a time." How she adored Dietrich back then.

He was so superstitious. Believed if he prayed for one hour without blinking, he'd have an apparition of the Blessed Mother, who'd bring him a cat that wouldn't make him sick. He kept praying. But cats thickened his breath, made him cough. Elmar got sick from cats, too. But Thekla didn't. Dietrich also believed that going into the synagogue or the Protestant church was a mortal sin. That's why Thekla didn't tell him when Herr Abramowitz took her inside the synagogue where the air was soft and cool. The day after the synagogue, she and Dietrich found a cat. The cat was drinking. Drinking steadily in the hot sun. Crouched by the blade of a fallen shovel, it was drinking from the water in that blade, its reflection surrounded by Dietrich's reflection.

Sobbing—

Not Dietrich, no—

Someone in her classroom. She thought it was empty.

Bruno. Still at his desk. Sobbing, a quiet sobbing. When she takes his hands, he resists, stiffly. He has his father's dainty hands. But on him they're in proportion to his body. Cold, his hands. So cold.

She opens them. On his palms, half-moon impressions of his fingernails. "What's wrong, Bruno?"

His lips are as pale as his face. He's shaking.

"I'll go with you to the nurse's office," she says.

He tries to speak.

"Bruno. Please tell me?"

He looks devastated, skin stretched, ears flat, as if standing in a strong wind.

"Did something happen?" Fear rises in her, and she takes his face between her hands. Her fingertips meet in back of his neck. His shorn hair feels like three-day beard fuzz where it ends above his soft winter-skin.

"I can't live without the Führer," he sobs.

"Oh, Bruno . . ." Why does he have to be so dramatic? "Sshhh . . . I'll talk to your parents about how important it is for you to be in the Hitler-Jugend."

But he only cries harder.

"Bruno? Listen to me."

"If you tell—"

"I'll be careful."

"—*Vati* will nail my window shut and I'll never get out."

He throws his arms around her middle and his entire body is drumming against her, his belly and muscles, his face in the dip between her breasts as if he wanted to burrow into her, hide, and she will remember his face, there, so cold she feels it through her dress—remember just a few hours later when his father will cling to her, howling, his body, too, drumming against her.

Chapter 22

"WE'LL BE THE first school in the district to announce our plans for celebrating the Führer's birthday," Sister Mäuschen is saying when Thekla rushes into the faculty meeting.

"I'm sorry I'm late." She raises her right arm, still shaken from what just happened with Bruno. "Heil Hitler."

The sisters and teachers around the library table raise their right arms. "Heil Hitler."

"One of my students had a problem and needed—"

"Sit down, please." Sister Josefine leans toward Sister Mäuschen. "But his birthday is still two months away."

"May I please remind you of the Führer's last birthday?" asks Sister Mäuschen, usually so shy she nibbles her words before anyone can hear. But whenever she mentions the Führer, her voice fills out. "That's when Dr. Goebbels told us how destiny chose the Führer from the masses because of his purity and his brilliance. God gave him this honorary post in history so the whole world can celebrate him." Sister Mäuschen swallows. Tucks her chapped hands into her sleeves, relapsing into the obedient little mouse. She used to be a spirited child, so stubborn about not liking shoes that she'd bury them whenever her mother made her wear them.

"Every one of our students should memorize the Führer's poem about his mother. *'Mutter'* is the title." As Sister Mäuschen recites it, her voice deepens into that of a man rhapsodizing about his mother's beloved devoted eyes: *wenn ihre lieben treuen Augen nicht mehr wie einst ins Leben sehn;* about his mother's feet, which have grown tired and don't want to carry her anymore while she walks: *wenn ihre müd' gewordnen Füsse sie nicht mehr tragen woll'n beim Gehn*—

Do his mother's eyes go first? Thekla wonders. Or her feet?

Across the table from her, the school nurse, Sister Agathe, is doing her best not to laugh by pressing her thumbs into the corners of her mouth to keep it level. Her little face, tucked inside her wimple and veil, is bright pink.

". . . ending with the harsh hour," Sister Mäuschen continues, "when his mother's mouth no longer asks him for anything: *die Stunde kommt, die bittre Stunde, da dich ihr Mund nach nichts mehr frägt.*

*

A bad poet, Thekla thinks. He failed as a painter. Tried to write opera, wanting to be another Wagner. And now these congested rhymes that would have never made it into the Echtermeyer collection. In art, sentimentality is not only insincere but unforgivable.

Why doesn't Sister Josefine say anything? She knows good poetry. Is she afraid of Sister Mäuschen? What would Sister Mäuschen say if she knew Thekla still has Fräulein Siderova's Echtermeyer? Last fall, when the list of banned books kept growing, Thekla thought it unwise to keep the poetry collection on her school desk. She carried it home, planning to bring it to Fräulein Siderova. A reason to visit. But she was afraid she'd intrude. Yet, the longer she waited, the more she imagined conversations with her teacher.

Better make a book cover for the Echtermeyer from butcher paper or conceal it inside the linen book jacket her mother embroidered. By now the black list has almost three thousand titles. Vera Inber's works are on that list. Lion Feuchtwanger's. Heinrich Mann's. Stefan Zweig's. Kurt Tucholsky's. But there are enough other German poets whose books are not banned. Goethe is magnificent *and* a safe choice. So is Annette von Droste-Hülshoff. Theodor Storm, too. And definitely Friedrich von Schiller.

I can do this as long as they let me teach. Stretching into this—*I can do this*—Thekla looks straight at Sister Mäuschen. "I appreciate your focus on Mother's Day," she says, "because I've already considered my lesson plan." She has not thought of a lesson plan, much less of the Führer's birthday, but then the word *consider* can be intended to mean the possibility of thought.

"So what is it you are considering?" Fräulein Buttgereit asks her, mouth set in the familiar lines of disappointment that square her chin. Her parents won't let her get engaged to the driver of the bakery truck, Alfred Meyer, who's courted her for years without having one moment alone with her.

"In the weeks leading up to *Muttertag,*" Thekla answers, "my students and I will collect early spring flowers and—"

"My goal, all along," Fräulein Buttgereit interrupts, "has been to impress on my students how the Führer loves them."

Pathetic, Thekla thinks. That's why boys like Bruno think they can't live without him. "My goal," she says, "is to make the theme of the German *Mutter* the focus of all subjects: history, geography, art . . . including botany and handwriting."

*

She's making up details as she talks, before any of the other teachers can. If she has to, she can be more patriotic than any of them. She knows what they say about her—that she's ambitious—but if they'd waited ten years for a teaching job, they'd be ambitious, too.

Still, no one is more ambitious than Sister Josefine. Especially when it comes to self-denial. Austerity has been seductive for the sister, the Spartan training of her body rewarding her with ascetic zeal. And yet, her healthy teeth betray her privileged upbringing. Winning, people say about her, she is good at winning. Riding in competitions as a young woman. As girls, Thekla and her classmates whispered that Sister Josefine lost her hymen bouncing on a horse. Already they could tell that nuns had more power than married women.

"Each student," Thekla says to Sister Mäuschen, "will compose a poem for his *Mutter* and copy it in his best handwriting, and—"

"Excellent idea, Fräulein Jansen."

But Sister Josefine watches quietly, gauging what's real and what's politics for the new teacher, who's intelligent but self-indulgent. That silk scarf of hers . . . tied so low that her clavicle shows. *Vain.* But at least in good taste.

"—and he'll decorate the poem with pressed flowers from our botany lesson," Thekla Jansen continues and thinks of pressing flowers with Fräulein Siderova. *Remember that hike to the flour mill, Fräulein? You took us across fields toward the faraway sun that burned through the mist yellow-white as we collected flowers to press for our bookmarks.* Teichrosen *glistened on the pond's flatness, and around its bank* Löwenzähnchen—*snapdragons and* Hahnenfuss—*buttercups crowded each other. In the grass the blue of forget-me-nots. Birds gaudy in elderberry trees, in apple trees, twitter and bloom everywhere. Meadows. And then the brick arches of the flour mill. Purple thistles. An anthill. Under the umbrella leaves of the* Holunder *we settled down with you. That fox we saw—sleek and red and low; then another, smaller;*

another yet. And bees, diving into petals and emerging covered with yellow dust.

Always, that solace in nature. That's what Thekla wants for her boys, too. Suddenly she has an idea. This afternoon she'll take them to the Rhein for their lessons, even if the rain picks up again. They'll be excited, eager to be outdoors. Already, she can feel that sensation of walking in the rain, face tilted up, clothes molded to her. But that was summer rain. She smiles to herself.

Sister Mäuschen smiles back as if waiting to hear more.

*

Gisela Stosick has stood outside the school for ten minutes, shivering in the damp wind while students spilled from the double door, greeting her, "*Guten Tag,* Frau Stosick," as they headed home. Her feet are cold despite her new ankle boots, embossed leather the color of cognac. It makes her sad that most of these students don't own boots, just shoes, worn shoes. Her son has two pairs of shoes and two pairs of boots. Good quality and waterproofed. Not every child is that lucky.

If she had more children, she wouldn't be able to buy Bruno new boots whenever he needed them. She and Günther certainly wanted more. "God's will," Herr Pastor Schüler consoled her, while she dreamed of strangling God. Three times she imagined yanking God from his throne in his heaven, once for each child pulled dead from her womb. Until she had Bruno and it would have been foolish to provoke God.

When Gisela goes inside the school to find Bruno, his classroom is empty. Briefly, she lays one flat hand against the top of the desk—smooth from centuries of children's hands—where she sat as a girl, right behind Thekla Jansen, who used to be Fräulein Siderova's favorite. Knowing all the answers. Volunteering to clean the chalkboard.

Thekla will know where Bruno is.

Gisela goes to find her in the teachers' lounge, knocks at the door, knocks again, and opens it halfway. "I'm sorry to interrupt. I'm searching for Bruno. Oh— Heil Hitler."

"Heil Hitler," Sister Mäuschen says.

"Bruno went home," Thekla Jansen says. "He stayed behind for a little while after the other boys left, but then he went home, too."

*

But Gisela Stosick is already retreating, closing the door quietly. The rain has let up, and the sky is getting lighter. As she rushes home, she tells herself Bruno must have sneaked out the back of the school to avoid the embarrassment of his mother waiting for him. Her independent boy who used to walk home by himself. She must talk with Günther, remind him how happy it made Bruno to see her once he got home, how he'd tell her and his father about his morning while they ate lunch. She misses how it used to be.

She has no doubts about protecting her son from Hitler's propaganda, but she's not all that sure, anymore, if keeping him out of the Hitler-Jugend is best for him. It makes him even more different than other boys. He's bright and shy, the target of bullies. Some of her friends think she's foolish. They say the regime will spin itself out.

The instant she enters her house through the side door, she hears something falling in the living room.

"Bruno?"

He must have arrived home before her. Again, she calls his name. Opens the door to the living room partway. No one there. And it was more like a bumping sound than a fall, really.

In the kitchen, she mashes boiled potatoes and apples, *Himmel und Erde*—heaven and earth, a good winter dish, potatoes from the Weinharts' delivery last fall and apples she and Bruno picked at the little orchard in Krefeld. She stores them in her cellar on shelves lined with newspapers, and they're a bit puckered by now; still, they taste fresh whenever she stirs them together, *Himmel und Erde,* mingling the flavors of what was grown close to heaven and in the earth.

*

"My students already memorize one poem each week," Thekla says. "Poems appropriate to the seasons . . . poems about loss or celebration . . . and they write their own, about a person or a pet they love. I plan to expand on that by leading my boys into a discussion of poems about their mothers."

Sister Mäuschen nods, pleased.

So far, Thekla feels, she's been navigating through the meeting quite well. She says, "That discussion is bound to generate goodwill because my students will tell their parents and their group leaders. Scholastically it'll inspire them to talk about their own *Mutter.*"

"It's our responsibility as teachers," Sister Josefine says, "to respect that creative urge in each child, to do all we can to let it unfold. Are there any other suggestions?" She glances around, at her sisters and teachers.

Most don't care for the government and are appropriately discreet; but a few are outdoing one another with how they'll incorporate the Führer and his poetry into their lesson plans.

To impress her principal, Fräulein Talmeister talks about *turnen*—exercising with the children. Everyone knows Sister Josefine supports the government's rigorous training that wipes out laziness in the souls of the young. "Physical exercise," Fräulein Talmeister starts, "used to be perceived as being just for the individual . . . the strengthening of the body, the habit of discipline. But I've realized that this is selfish." She fusses with the sailor collar of her striped blouse. "The Führer teaches us that exercise is our duty for our country."

Exercising for the Führer. Really. Thekla wants to laugh but keeps her face impassive. She can stay outside all of that. But just then she remembers the rally when, just for an instant, she felt part of it. Like touching a flame but getting burned instead and feeling tricked. Though she shook herself free from that spell and returned to who she believed she was, she felt agitated for days. But if she has to, she'll tell her students that the Führer wants them to exercise more. If that makes their lives easier while the regime lasts. *But bad poetry? Never.*

"The body is a temple of the Holy Spirit," Sister Mäuschen says enthusiastically. "We must prepare our students to be able-bodied citizens and soldiers who'll sacrifice for the Vaterland."

*

But Sister Josefine is not about to speak of children as soldiers. She brings the discussion back to what matters, the teaching.

"During my art lesson," Thekla says, "my students will learn how to make bookmarks from their poems and the flowers they picked. We'll wrap each bookmark in tissue paper and weigh it down with books. After a day or two, we'll use a clear sealer. I still have a bookmark I made here as a girl."

Sudden winds bend the treetops outside the window. Then it is calm again, with the sky almost white and the trees black sticks against that white sky. She wonders how Bruno is.

"I like to combine all subjects within the process of learning," Thekla continues. "Biology and music and literature and mathematics. All at once. So that the connections between the subjects become as significant as the subjects themselves."

I wish I could tell them that this is your philosophy, Fräulein Siderova, but that would be foolish. It's best for our students that I continue your way of teaching.

"That unity in teaching," Sister Mäuschen says, "is exactly what the Führer wants from us as educators."

Thekla opens her lips, stunned. How dare Sister twist what she said to validate the Führer's ideas about education? His grammar in *Mein Kampf* is atrocious, a poor example for students. No excuse that he wrote it in prison.

Sister Mäuschen is waiting.

Thekla wonders if saying nothing means she's expected to say yes to everything from now on. *Shouldn't you be safe going along with the nuns, your conscience and all taken care of? No. I didn't start any of this. Once the regime wears itself down, I'll get back to my own moral compass, to who I was before. And I'll lobby for you to come back and teach, Fräulein Siderova. As soon as you enter my—*

As soon as you enter our classroom, you notice what I've changed to advance our boys, and what I've kept unchanged to honor you.

"The position is yours again," I tell you.

"I can't take this from you."

But I insist. "You're not taking anything from me. It has always been yours."

"But what about you, Thekla? What will you do?"

"I've been offered another position . . . as assistant principal."

"Where?"

In Oberkassel— No. Neuss? Why not here in Burgdorf, at this school where I can look after you? "Right here in Burgdorf," I tell you.

You tell me I'm gracious. "Very gracious," you say.

Chapter 23

WHEN THEY GET READY to leave the schoolhouse, Monika Buttgereit buttons her plaid coat. As usual, she's wearing too many colors. *Vulgar.* Her family's house is like that, too, shelves and tables crammed with every item they own.

"Now she has taken in a boarder," she whispers to Thekla.

"Who?"

"Fräulein Siderova."

"I doubt that."

"It's a fact. I heard about it from Trudi Montag."

Thekla pauses. Any gossip coming through Trudi Montag is reliable. She feels oddly hurt. If she'd known Fräulein Siderova was open to boarders, she would have asked to rent from her years ago.

Fräulein Buttgereit's eyes are bright, curious. "She can no longer afford a *Putzfrau*—cleaning woman."

Putzfrau? For an instant Thekla thinks it's her mother Monika Buttgereit is talking about. But her mother is not a *Putzfrau*. She's a housekeeper. Even though she does clean the Abramowitzes' house. But that's just part of her job. She also cooks and irons and—

With both hands, Monika Buttgereit lifts her elaborate hat concoction and lowers it on her hair. Feathers and pom-poms.

A boarder . . . Maybe the artist who painted Fräulein Siderova's oil portrait aboard that ship to Jerusalem is now living with her—still is her lover—and she's only saying he's a boarder to make it look proper. *After the ship returned, he couldn't forget you and searched for you, Fräulein Siderova. How would he have found you? By asking for the passenger list? How long ago would that have been, Fräulein Siderova? Perhaps he saw you get on a train in Düsseldorf? Not on a train, no. He didn't see you for many years, but a few months ago the two of you met again at a gallery opening. In Düsseldorf. Where you recognized the other painting he'd done of you—yes, that's how: he did two paintings and kept one, and when you turned, he was standing behind you and you didn't have to speak because you knew you would always be together from now on—*

*

As Thekla hastens toward her parents' house, her shoes squeak on the snow. Tuesday lunch is always rushed because of the faculty meeting. There is a thickness to the light, and on the front steps of the pay-library, the Montags' dog is sleeping, his fur pale gray except for his head, a mask of dark gray.

She feels someone watching her. Helmut Eberhardt. Standing in the doorway of the grocery store. At thirteen, he is already taller than the teacher. Not a single crease in his uniform. He joined the Hitler-Jugend last year, right after the Führer announced on the radio that he wanted to double the membership. When Helmut was an altar boy, Frau Brocker liked to say she just knew that he would become a priest, that he was an angel come to earth, so handsome, so helpful.

"Heil Hitler," Frau Brocker's angel says to Thekla and raises his arm. Long sleeves, but most people know about the scar beneath the brown fabric.

The teacher has seen the scar only once, after he competed in a *Langstreckenlauf*—long-distance run and raised his trophy, exposing the scarred length of silvery skin.

"Heil Hitler," she responds.

At the Abramowitzes' house across the street, the shutters are closed, the window boxes empty. Come summer, they'll be filled with purple geraniums and snapdragons. She wonders if Frau Abramowitz still reads those trashy novels from the pay-library. As a child Thekla could feel that current—from Frau Abramowitz, not from Herr Montag—and now she suspects it has less to do with the books than with the man who lends the books.

If he were to sell shoes, say, or bread, Frau Abramowitz and many other women in Burgdorf would be there, buying, just to be near him. In these women, he fosters a certain longing that evokes memories of other longings, the cool length of a thigh, say, or the sweet exhalation just after a kiss. When they come to his pay-library, he'll recommend books just right for them, that day, that hour. They'll touch his sleeve or pat his hand for as long as it's still proper, tell him what a good father he is to the daughter who caused his wife to lean across the edge of sanity. Granted, that edge was frail before, but Gertrud Montag managed to step back from it until she gave birth to the girl with a large head and short limbs. Such heartache for one man, the women will say. A widower since the dwarf girl was four. His son stillborn. His wife dead soon after. One carved cross with a little roof on their grave.

The women of Burgdorf don't worry that Leo will take advantage of their longing. He respects that the longing is theirs alone, protects himself from its burden with that very respect. But he does it with such kindness that women don't feel spurned and men can't possibly feel jealous; it's rather that the men learn from Leo and approach their women with puzzled courtesy.

*

"May I carry your satchel?" Helmut asks Fräulein Jansen. Always polite. The manners of a man. The urgency of a man.

She's used to that. "Thank you," she says.

Helmut shoulders her satchel, proud to be seen with her. As they set off, he squints at the mezuzah that hangs by the Abramowitzes' door. Thekla feels a flicker of caution. It could be a trap. Why provoke the rough elements of the party? If the Führer were to ask her counsel—not that he would, but if—she'd tell him he's achieved so much, he can let down on this heat against the Jews. Once he acknowledged to himself the value of the employment he'd created, she'd get him to focus on that, and it would only follow that he'd want to give up those crazy ideas about Jews. Not that she would use the word *crazy*. She'd be tactful.

To distract Helmut from the mezuzah, she touches his shoulder. "Has your arm been healing?"

He blushes hard. "I don't feel it anymore."

He and several other boys in the Hitler-Jugend chafed their arms raw with a pillowcase they knotted, hard, and rubbed up and down their arms till they were bleeding. While their mothers were mortified by their violence toward their bodies, Thekla understood that this was what boys did. They competed to prove their men-courage in boy-ways; tested their bodies' resilience to pain; and yet, they were childish in what they used, not weapons or stones but a pillowcase from home, warning off communists, wanting their courage noticed. *Boys.* She knows them better than their parents know them.

Chapter 24

When Thekla enters her parents' kitchen, *Vati* sits by the stove and *Mutti* has lunch ready from what she cooked at the Abramowitzes' today, goulash and potatoes in two covered pots that she lifts from the pail.

Outside on the washline, frost has stiffened the laundry, and *Vati*'s white shirt moves as one solid piece in the wind, the sleeves no longer flapping, no longer promising movement. If only she could shake it till his soul flew out and slipped back into his body.

"*Vati?* Are you hungry?"

Food is one of the few pleasures left to him, and she coaxes him until he blinks as if surfacing. His eyes fasten on *Mutti,* suddenly lucid, as she arranges the potatoes and meat on the platter she used for serving pigeons, a small center with a large rim to make the birds seem bigger.

But all the pigeons have been eaten or are with Elmar now.

Last summer he borrowed the potato truck from his employer,

lured the pigeons into cages, and transferred them to Kaiser Wilhelm Strasse, where he built a coop in the alley between his bedroom and the neighbor's house, so that he could watch the pigeons from his bed. But they kept flying back to their old coop until *Mutti* trained them to return to Elmar by refusing them food and water. She'd flap a tablecloth to chase them away, and when they'd arrive at Elmar's coop—with that indignant expression only pigeons have—he'd feed and water them, fuss over them.

*

As always, *Mutti* gets *Vati* started with lunch. "I've left a surprise in your room," she tells Thekla, who's eating quickly.

"I have to get back to work. Those faculty meetings don't leave me enough time to eat."

"At least look," *Mutti* says when they've cleared their plates, though *Vati* is still chewing, slowly. He's tidy when it comes to food.

"You'll be glad." *Mutti* stands up. "Come."

In Thekla's old room blossoms of mold—a thousand nuances of gray with amber and purple and white and green and red—have formed a fuzzy border beneath the frieze of Noah and his ark, a continuous band of the ark and Noah's wife and children and the animals—in pairs—walking up a plank to the ark; and then the ark again and the same long queue waiting to be saved. She still likes the gray more than the queue of animals, because it keeps changing in size and shape and color although, periodically, her mother scrubs it off.

On Thekla's bed is a small package, wrapped in the old flag, black, red, and gold.

"We're not supposed to keep that flag," Thekla says quickly.

"You know I don't waste things," her mother says. "Besides, I'm keeping it for when it comes back."

"It's not wise to tell people that."

"I'm telling you. Not people."

Thekla hesitates. Aesthetically the old flag is warmer, more pleasing than the new flag.

"What is it?" *Mutti* asks.

"The Abramowitzes' mezuzah—"

"Yes?"

"It would be safer to take it inside."

"I can't do that."

"Just for now."

"I'll mention it to them."

"I must get back to school."

"Open your present, Thekla."

"Can we do it tomorrow?"

Mutti nods.

In the kitchen, *Vati* is eating alone. Sundays they sit with him till he's finished, but weekdays she and *Mutti* rush back to work while he finishes for himself.

Thekla touches his sleeve. "I'll be back soon."

He moves his dry lips around what may become words, images, tunnels, deeper yet— But already the passage is slamming shut.

Because I don't love you enough?

1908

Chapter 25

THE AUGUST OF 1908, when Wilhelm Jansen took his young family to the Nordstrand peninsula as every summer, Thekla felt shy being away from home. While the little boys would scramble against their *Oma,* who smelled like a kitten, breath of milk, Thekla leaned into her father, who instinctively curved one arm around her.

He let her come along to the barn to get the cot and set it up between the two beds in his mother's room. Every summer his mother insisted he and his family sleep in her room while she moved into the narrow bedroom that used to be his. Every visit Wilhelm objected, though it pleased him that she'd want him to have the big room with the two beds.

When the little boys awoke before dawn, they climbed from the bed and across the cot where their sister was still asleep. In the other bed, their parents were spooning, *Mutti*'s lips against one wing of *Vati*'s shoulders, just as they slept in their bed at home.

*

Holding hands, the two boys searched for their *Oma*. In the kitchen, she was wrapping herself into a large shawl, and there was a blue dress beneath, bare feet.

She was undone by her hunger to caress Elmar and Dietrich, but she hesitated because touch would surely unleash the longing that felled her every summer after they left. Already, she had lost too many children. She had made a terrible mistake when she'd urged Wilhelm and Almut to leave Nordstrand, to get away from the gossip. It was only after they'd left that she realized how she must have hoped that they'd stay near her, that they'd be moved by her selfless gesture, that they'd remind her how she had withstood worse gossip. Yes, there were visits—Burgdorf at Christmas; Nordstrand in August—but they were not nearly enough for Lotte.

"Go back to bed," she said to her grandsons.

But already, and against all caution, she was enfolding them in her shawl, carrying them up the dike behind the house and down on the sea side, toward the moon. They curved themselves against her like any small mammals sharing warmth and breath—hers and each other's indistinguishable, warmth and breath and touch—and she wept silently because her arms were plenty to hold them both.

*

The little boys felt snug with their *Oma* in the dawn that was still almost black, but not all black, rather the kind of black that's tinged with blue when you know the blue will win; and the only bright light was that of the full moon till the shadow of earth began to slide across the moon, blackening it, and their *Oma* said it was an eclipse and showed them to watch for the sun rising on their other side, opposite of the black moon, and the boys watched hard, though the sun wasn't there yet, only the sky spreading rose-red flashes beyond the horizon, wide and muted flashes; suddenly, then, a tiny white flare, igniting into a red pinpoint, red and then the size of an apple, growing fast and becoming sun, rising from the sea into a half circle, a three-quarter circle above the edge of water and sky.

"Elmar," she said, "Dietrich," tasting the sounds of their names as the sun separated from the sea.

From his *Oma*'s arms, Dietrich could see the path that came from the sun across the water and lay on the tidal flats, golden, and he knew he wanted to live here. Become a priest. Or maybe a monkey trainer at the Zirkus. He slipped his fingers into his pocket. Curled them around the carved monkey the man from the Zirkus had given him when he'd come to the farm to eat with them.

"When is the Zirkus?" Dietrich asked, and when *Oma* said she had free tickets for tomorrow afternoon, he felt aglow with anticipation of real monkeys and tightrope walkers and clowns.

Oma pointed to the path on the water. It was as wide as the sun climbing into the sky. "Next summer," she said, "that path will be here for you again."

*

Wilhelm Jansen was proud of his daughter—how articulate she was, how polite—and he liked being a father, liked being seen walking with his daughter to the bakery to buy *Brötchen*—rolls for his entire family: his wife and his children and his mother. Before his sons were born, he'd fretted he might love Thekla less once he had children of his own; but that hadn't happened because it was from her, after all, that he had learned how to be a father, and his love for her continued though she had the best of everything while her brothers were poor. With three children, Wilhelm had less for each, but it was important to him to provide for them equally, and to have Thekla understand that, although the lawyer Abramowitz gave her far more.

Inside the bakery, smells of marzipan and yeast. Thekla pulled him to the glass display: Florentines, and chocolate tarts, and his wife's favorite, *Bienenstich*—bee sting, those layers of cake and custard and glazed almonds.

"Let's get *Bienenstich* for this afternoon," he said casually, as if this were something he did every Sunday for his family.

That bliss in his daughter's face. She drew in her lower lip as if already tasting it.

"It'll be a surprise from you and me." Already he could imagine other Sundays like this. From now on he'd be returning for more frequent visits to Nordstrand.

Whispering . . . the baker and one of the customers.

Thekla could make out the word *Kuckuck*—cuckoo. If you forgot to close your window, *Kuckucks* stole shiny things from your windowsill, wedding rings or baby spoons. In school she'd learned a song about the *Kuckuck* in the forest. She sang, *"Kuckuck, Kuckuck ruft's aus dem Wald—"*

But *Vati*'s hand closed around her wrist, and he pulled her from the bakery.

Without buying *Bienenstich* ? *Oh—*

"Don't listen to them." Breath high in *Vati*'s voice.

To keep his voice from flying away?

"You are mine!" Breath higher yet in *Vati*'s voice. "Just like your brothers."

Tuesday, February 27, 1934

Chapter 26

INSIDE ECKART'S LEFT EAR, the wad of cotton is cold, unyielding, but all around it, he feels the pain, hot and puffy, trying to shove out the cotton.

"Watch your step, Eckart," his teacher calls.

Franz and Andreas imitate his stumbling, hop around, nudge each other.

"Look at me, Fräulein."

"Look at me!"

"Watch your step, Eckart," they shout in their teacher's voice. And giggle.

The boys have been antsy ever since they came in from lunch and she told them to keep their coats buttoned to the collar, to wear their hats and their mittens, because she was taking them on a field trip. Impatient to start out, they didn't like waiting for Bruno.

Maybe Bruno is still feeling sick, the teacher thinks as they head up Römer Strasse and pass St. Martin's. Maybe Gisela is taking him right now to Frau Doktor Rosen.

*

By the Rathaus, Wolfgang points to a huge nest, twigs and dry leaves, propped in the highest fork of the chestnut tree.

"What kind of bird?" Richard asks.

"Squirrels," Wolfgang says. "I saw two of them build it last fall. One was arranging the nest. The other climbed higher and tore off a small branch. Then it hung upside down and gave the branch to the other squirrel, who added it to the nest."

"I've seen that," Richard says.

"We have a stuffed squirrel in our living room," Andreas says.

As they pass the slaughterhouse, some of the students mimic the squealing of hogs. The farm boys in Fräulein Jansen's class have seen plenty of animals die, but the boys from educated families try not to think about what goes on inside the slaughterhouse, yet they can't keep from picturing how those hogs and cows are killed—not killed right away but stunned first, hammer blows to their heads before their throats are slit. But they don't know that for sure. They could ask Walter, whose father works in the slaughterhouse, and in whose family that job is ordinary, talked about at the dinner table; but they don't dare ask and let real pictures of slaughter into their heads because those may be bloodier than what already haunts the boys' imagination.

They can't admit this, of course, and so they swagger and laugh, alongside the farm boys, who feel invincible as they make the brainy boys squirm.

"In there, they kill them in two seconds."

"They make the animals stand in a gutter—"

"So the blood runs from there into a vat."

"For *Blutwurst*—blood sausage."

"Moo . . ."

"And the animals stomp around to make the *Wurst*—"

"Until they fall over . . . ."

*

On the river side of the dike, clumps of winter-dry grasses sway in the breeze. Fallen branches lie bleached from sun and rain. The boys find gnawed bones in a crevice of roots, a blackened fire pit that someone has built from stones. As they hunker and observe, they feel the learning seep into their bodies like breath, almost, or like soul, a shape they can't describe but know is there, just as they know from their teacher that learning lives inside them with all they have learned before, ready to connect to more learning. During the cold weeks to come, inside their classroom, they'll reach for those experiences, deepen them, remind one another of all they know about the world that surrounds them.

When they identify bare trees according to bark and formation of branches, Franz says, "They're all alike in winter."

"Not if you know what to check for," Wolfgang says.

Franz kicks at a punky branch, and it flies into dust.

"Franz," their teacher says, "has swallow nests in his barn." She motions to the swallows that flit in high arcs above, then dip against the surface of the river. "Maybe he'll tell us how they get their food."

"They screech and open their beaks," Franz says, "as soon as their parents bring them mosquitoes or flies, and every spring our nests are full of young ones."

"Will you show us in the spring?" she asks.

He nods eagerly.

"We'll make an excursion to your barn," she says.

And that's when Franz remembers what he learned about bark at the Sternburg farm, which used to be a fortress. By the moat, she chose a birch, an oak, a chestnut, and a poplar. Assigned several boys to each tree. Showed them how to press paper against a section of bark and, pencil at an angle, rub the lead across the paper till the pattern of the bark stood out. Then the work in the classroom: sketching the details of the bark, writing an essay to describe the bark. His project was the best. Franz could tell by the way his teacher nodded when he showed it to her.

Suddenly he wants her to know that he remembers. "Bark only seems the same from one day to the next."

"You're right," she says. "It's because we only notice seasonal changes."

"Except the changing is happening every second," he says.

*

Jochen Weskopp has fallen behind. That's how he must be on his way to school, the teacher thinks, dawdling. Still, that's what he needs: he gets as much from his quiet observation as from any teacher. How to give him both? She waits for him by a stand of poplars.

"Feel how springy the ground is?" He raises himself on his toes, rocks back on his heels.

She bounces, lightly. "You're right. Why do you think it is like that?"

"From all those layers of leaves."

"Our future biologist."

"I want to be a soldier."

"You told me you want to be a biologist."

"No. A hero," he tells her, as if certain of her approval.

"How about afterward?"

"Afterward?"

"You can be a biologist then."

He tips his child-face toward her. "Afterward I'll be dead."

"Don't say that!"

Grown and dead, Jochen, his grave, and his mother on her knees—

Thekla shivers. How devastating it must be for parents to lose a son whose features have not matured into his man-face, who will forever evoke the infant. *Aus Kindern werden Soldaten*—children become soldiers.

"We don't want another war," she says abruptly. "You are too young, Jochen."

*

By the river it's all gray sky and gray water. A thin ice ledge rises from the water, and below that ledge, layers of sand and vegetation stick from the snow. Across the current lies a strip of sand and above it a strip of rounded tree silhouettes like paper cutouts.

The boys race for the old willow trees whose trunks have been flooded again and again, leaving rippled watermarks around their bark. As the boys climb, their bodies darken the bare limbs and rock the whippy branches that reach for their reflections in the current.

These willows had leaves when we were here with you, Fräulein Siderova. Remember that race you did with us? I came in third, and you braided a crown of wildflowers for the winner.

Suddenly Thekla is experiencing it all at once—the cold air that surrounds her and that long-ago sun coming through—and she feels warmer. She pushes up her sleeves, slips off her gloves. As a girl she climbed willows, and she still prefers nature over exercise equipment. Far more exciting to leap across a ditch than across a rope, to do chin-ups on a strong branch than on a steel rod. She has always been athletic. Started to walk when she was only eight months old. It made her more daring, knowing that about herself.

*

Eckart staggers, pushes his finger into his ear to stop the ache where the pain is squeezing the cotton wad.

Several boys mimic his staggering.

"Boys," the teacher says. Usually one glance will do. The more the students love you, the less you need to remind them to behave.

"Eckart is drooling," Andreas sings out.

"Stop it," Eckart cries, sleeve to his mouth. Edge of scarf unraveling.

But a chant has already started: "Eckart drools like Gerda Heidenreich . . . Eckart drools like Gerda Heidenreich . . ."

And for an instant, there, just before Eckart starts to hate Gerda, he's stunned by compassion for her: Gerda, whose neck is slick with drool, whose face and body twitch.

Laughter.

Little-boy-bawdy laughter.

While the teacher is remembering how Frau Abramowitz smiled at Gerda. It makes the teacher's belly cramp as it did when she was fifteen and, late one afternoon, picked up her mother from work and found Frau Abramowitz with the Montags' newborn dwarf girl in her arms, singing to her. Smiling.

*

" . . . drools like Gerda Heidenreich . . ."

Eckart stumbles into sky that's suddenly upside down, skins his palms on mud flecked with granules of leftover snow.

"Stop it, boys. Now." The teacher has stopped it before, this pattern of one child being singled out, bullied.

"Gerda Heidenreich drools from her lips."

"From where else would she drool?"

"From her *Arschloch*—asshole."

They're startled by their audacity.

Giddy because their teacher is not able to break them up.

Between Eckart's palms is a glazed puddle, amber leaves suspended beneath delicate ice that crackles, splinters, as he raises himself on his knees.

"Boys!" Thekla maneuvers herself between him and the boys.

But they don't budge. Their sudden scorn is so palpable that, any moment now, they may turn on her, no longer individual boys she can guide but a pack. Her palms are wet, and it comes to her how, with the government, too, she believed she could manage it, yet once unleashed, it was overtaking her, all of them. Across the river, people are no more than dots, unable to help even if they were to recognize the danger. And what Thekla knows instinctively is this: *If you step back, you are lost. The urge of the pack will escalate.*

Chapter 27

JUST THEN, OTTO separates himself from the knot of boys, comes toward his teacher, crouches next to Eckart. She's afraid the others will assail him, too. But the consistency of the pack has been altered and is breaking up into separate boys who disperse to kick roots or point at the barges that lie low in the current.

After arising from a dream that still mortifies them, a dream so ancient, so entrancing, they don't dare look at one another. *We could have feasted on her. Now that she has seen us like this, nothing can be as before.*

As Otto brushes debris from Eckart's patched coat, the teacher thinks of talking with him about Bruno. He'd watch out for Bruno—to please her, quite likely—but it would be good for both if a friendship were to come out of it. Tomorrow, she thinks and pulls all her boys into her gaze, steady, steady, until they are still.

"Tell me what you see," she demands and points to a barge that's slowly heading upstream near the bank.

The boys eye her with caution.

She waits out their silence.

"This one is empty," Richard finally says. "That's why it's in the shallow part of the river."

"A good observation," she praises him. "Please, tell us how you know."

"It sits high in the water. That means it's on the way to get loaded up again."

"Excellent."

"Barges that are loaded," Andreas volunteers, "are deep in the water. That's why they need to be where it's deep."

"Very good." She feels herself gaining control by encouraging them to teach one another. "What else can you tell us—all of you?"

"Deep water is in the middle of the river," Franz says.

"And to keep those channels open," the teacher adds, "a special barge dredges the bottom from time to time."

"But when they're empty like this barge, they don't need to be in the middle," Richard says.

Franz nods. "They can float close to the bank where it's shallow."

"Just think how your parents must have stood here and figured this out when they were your age."

"Our grandparents, too."

*

Across the river the ferry is docking, bright yellow. Everything else is gray and white, including the seagulls.

"A story from you, Fräulein," Otto says.

She usually has new stories for them on their learning excursions, and they know how much she enjoys the telling.

"A scary story," Andreas says. "Please?"

I could really scare you. The stories I could tell you . . . The scariest story came from the Bible. Abraham, the worst of all fathers, listening to the voice of God. How could that fit in with listening to your con-

science, if your conscience was the voice of God? More likely Abraham was just another lunatic, seeking his logic in God. Because how else could he justify his readiness to kill his child? My father would have been too weak to listen to God. He wouldn't have lifted his hands from his knees—

Which father?

—*Nein nein jetzt nicht. Weg damit*—No no not now. Away with this—

"I have a ghost story," Walter says and waits for the teacher to nod to him. "Once upon a time in old times, there was a decrepit old farmer who lived in Burgdorf. One night, one foggy, foggy night . . . he went out in his oxcart. It was foggy—"

"You already said it was foggy," Richard interrupts.

"—very foggy. And the decrepit old farmer couldn't see where he was going, and all at once a ghost was sitting next to him—"

"The ghost of his decrepit old teacher?" Thekla asks.

Her boys laugh aloud.

"We have someone in my family," Franz says, "who turned into a cloud and flew away on a chicken and her name was Sabine and she was—"

"You can tell us after Walter finishes his story," Thekla says.

"I'm done," Walter says. "I want to hear Franz's story."

"First you have to say 'the end.'"

"The end."

"Sabine was my grandfather's little sister," Franz says, "and when she was five years old, her mother told her to play quietly in her room, but Sabine was disobedient and sneaked outside to search for her pet chicken, and the chicken turned into a cloud and flew off with Sabine, who also turned into a cloud, and they were never seen again. The end."

*

"Tell us a story, Fräulein."

"I have a story for you. A story in a poem. '*Et wassen twee Künigeskinner . . .*'"

Her boys tell her they can't understand her.

"It's not real German," they say.

"Oh, but it is German . . . as it was spoken hundreds of years ago. Even today, our language is spoken in different dialects." She smiles at Heinz, who rubs his knobby wrists. "And it's good for us to know more than one dialect."

She can see that he suddenly feels ahead of the other students, confident that he knows more than they do. Her exhilaration at his progress is what she believes love is: to bring her students forward and to release them once they're ready. They weren't hers to start out with.

"Listen now," she says.

> *"Et wassen twee Künigeskinner,*
> *De hadden enanner so lef—"*

"That's not German."

"Fräulein!"

"Yes, it is. Our language is always changing, depending on the times we live in, the region we live in. It's a song you already know. I'll give you a hint." She hums the song about the two *Königskinder*—royal children who loved each other but could not come together because the water between their castles was far too deep.

Heinz starts humming along.

You should see him, Fräulein Siderova, that smile of his—from reluctant to full force—there's no in between for him. He'll give his heart away with that smile.

Soon all her boys are humming and singing with her about the *Königskinder* who yearned to be together.

"Es waren zwei Königskinder,
Die hatten einander so lieb,
Sie konnten zusammen nicht kommen,
Das Wasser war viel zu tief."

*

"So many ways of taking language to tell a story," she tells her boys. "For centuries, poets have retold this story of the *Königskinder*. Artists have made sculptures of them, painted pictures."

Like an itch, then, remembering the poem of the Führer. An insult. To teach bad poetry is to betray herself and the sacred work of teaching. She feels outraged at having to do this. But not yet. She doesn't have to think about it till then.

She tells her boys the Greek legend of Hero and Leander, and they listen closely to how Ovid wrote about the young couple, and how the story passed through the ages to artists and writers all over the world who created their own versions of the ancient legend. Four hundred years ago it appeared in the German language. Much later—and yet still a hundred years ago—Annette von Droste-Hülshoff was writing about the *Königskinder*.

"You, too, can make that story yours," Thekla says. "Think about someone you yearn to be with but can't—the reason doesn't matter, just that you can't. And then imagine how you'll tell that story . . . in a drawing, or with words, or with music."

"I'll draw a picture," Andreas says.

Franz wonders if he should write about Uncle Gustav, to whom his parents are no longer speaking.

Richard thinks about the father he never met and is forbidden to ask about. "Can you miss someone you don't know?" he asks.

"Like people who were dead before we were born?" Eckart asks him.

"Not dead," Richard snaps.

Gently, the teacher touches his wrist. "Of course you can miss someone like that."

He raises his face to her. "I know that."

Otto plans to write about his best friend ever, Markus, who lives on a cliff next to an amusement park in America where he'll take Otto when he goes to visit. He and Markus will ride the carousel together, count the skyscrapers across the Hudson River, which flows past the house where Markus's family lives with his Tante Trina.

*

Clouds move in front of the sun, and right away it gets chilly. To warm her boys, the teacher gets them to stomp their cold feet and flap their arms, pretending to be birds.

"I'm a swallow," she cries, her back to the dike.

"I'm an eagle."

"I'm a wild goose."

Wolfgang, the most athletic of Fräulein Jansen's boys, leaps the highest. "I'm a stork." Elaborate legwork—rising and stretching, the illusion of endless legs.

The boys laugh as fresh air streams through their lungs and they feel the strength that comes with it, the conviction that they can do anything. *Through the skin first.*

"Storks carry babies."

"*Ja,* Wolfgang. Babies."

"Not this stork!"

Spreading their arms, they hop and stomp and dance. They like the flatness of the land as they leap above it, only trees and the dike rising from that flatness, only one little figure scurrying along the crest of the dike, then down toward the river, slipping once, scrambling up again.

Chapter 28

GISELA STOSICK SEARCHES her house once again after her husband has gone to look for their son. She searches Bruno's room. Nothing. Then his teacher's apartment because Bruno likes to visit her. The teacher invites him inside, but she comes downstairs when she has something to say. *This is not snooping.* Gisela unlocks the door. Her hands are itching. *I have a reason to be here. The right to be here.* The teacher's rooms are tidy but comfortable. Tidy in the way you'd keep your home when you're expecting visitors. *Not me. She's not expecting me.* Inside, no evidence of Bruno. Or of the secrets her son brings here. Of that she is certain: that he no longer brings his secrets to her but to his teacher. With her fingertips, Gisela traces the carvings on a dark panel. It feels very old. Valuable. She picks up a pillow, strokes the embroidery. Obviously the stitching of the teacher's mother, who has used the full thickness of each thread, bright colors that rise from the cloth in bold patterns. No flowers or tiny animals for Almut Jansen.

All at once Gisela feels envious. This stitching is far more intricate than that on the tablecloth she bought from Almut Jansen at the Christmas market. *Only the best for Almut's daughter. Who takes it. Who knows how to make herself the favorite. Especially with Bruno. It has been such a mistake to rent to her.* When Gisela returns to her own living room, she finds chess books and chess clocks and boxes with chess pieces stacked against the wall behind the door. How odd. The club meets tonight, but usually the first members to arrive get everything from the birch wardrobe. Sometimes Günther starts setting up before the others get there, but he wouldn't leave this mess on the floor. Besides, he wasn't home long enough. Bruno must have done this. So he could hide inside the wardrobe. He and his hiding games.

*

By the river, the boys are hopping and stomping and dancing and some clowning around so their teacher will notice them. She, too, is leaping, laughing, her scarf rising with her, levitating above her for a second or two whenever she lands.

"I'm an ostrich. Look at me, Fräulein."

"Me, look at me. I'm bigger than an ostrich."

The teacher is facing her boys and the river, her back to the figure that scurries toward them, getting bigger, legs and arms pumping, suit jacket flapping around the belly.

Already, she's feeling warmer, and she can tell her boys are, too, because their faces are flushed, their voices enthusiastic as they call out the names of birds and mimic their flights. Like Fräulein Siderova, she has used this day to its best, has won sight and insight for her boys, has woven botany and linguistics and fairy tales, linking her students, once again, to the beauty of their *Heimat*—homeland. The learning excursion she took as a girl with Fräulein Siderova is blurring with today's—laughter and blossoms and birds and pine pitch and the new green of leaves.

Andreas is waving to someone behind her.

"It's Bruno's *Vater,*" Walter says.

*

Impatiently, Gisela walks toward the wardrobe where Bruno must be hiding, tilting his head in the dark, listening for her steps. She doesn't have time for this. But when she pictures that little mischievous smile of his, she stops herself. *Let him play. It's good for him. He doesn't play nearly enough.* If only she'd been able to give him brothers and sisters. From the day he could walk, he loved to hide from her. But only if she was nearby, playing her piano, say, or ironing, so he could count on her to find him. As he is counting on her to find him now. Far too grown-up in other ways. The clicking of the dog's toenails next to her.

*

Herr Stosick is running toward the teacher and her boys.

"How is Bruno?" she calls out to him.

Face red, he stops, bends forward, hands on his knees, his breath so jagged he can't speak.

Has he found out about Bruno climbing from the window at night? And that she hasn't reported it to him? And that she knows he's still a member of the Hitler-Jugend? Is that why he's kept Bruno from returning to school?

Is he going to tell her she has to move out of her apartment? She wants to cry at the unfairness of it. Already she misses her apartment. How unprofessional it would be of Herr Stosick to evict her in front of her students. She is teaching, and he should be at his school, doing his work. Instinctively, she steps between him and her boys, spreads her arms to contain them.

*

Gisela reaches down to rub Henrietta's thick neck. Just a few years ago Bruno was still small enough to ride the dog, hold on to her collar, saying politely, "Please, carry me to my room." But Henrietta wouldn't budge, not till Bruno slid off her back, and then she'd shake her broad head, specks of drool flying from her speckled jowls. The dog is rubbing herself against Gisela's left thigh, whimpering. "Enough," Gisela says. Tail straight up, Henrietta trots toward the wardrobe, and for an instant Gisela feels embarrassed for the dog with her rump exposed like that. Henrietta sniffs the door, whimpers again.

*

"Where have you been?" Herr Stosick's hair clings to his scalp, sweaty despite the cold.

"On a learning excursion. With my students."

"Bruno?" He moves past her into the midst of her boys like a swimmer, arms separating them, his bulk the size of three boys. "Bruno!"

"Herr Stosick, please!"

"Bruno!" His voice hoarse like a foghorn.

*

"What is this, Henrietta?" Gisela makes loud steps, for her son to hear. "Someone left out all the chess books. I'll put them back inside." No need to spoil Bruno's little game. There'll be enough time to eat and get him back to school.

*

The boys scowl as Bruno's father pushes them aside, then tighten into one circle around their teacher, solidify. She feels them shifting, three deep between her and Herr Stosick. It makes her uneasy though she knows they want to protect her. Even if they're back to normal, she isn't.

"We waited for Bruno," she says. "We—"

"Bruno?" Now he's circling her and the boys, herding them. "Where is he?"

They can taste their power, know they can shield one another from him. Even the new boy, Heinz, now belongs with them.

"Bruno is at home," Andreas shouts.

"At home," Heinz says, defiant.

*

Gisela taps the blond wood of the wardrobe. "I wonder where Bruno is?" she sings out. "Bruno . . . ?"

*

"We waited for Bruno before we moved our biology and art lessons outdoors," the teacher tells Herr Stosick.

"Your principal didn't know where you were! You and all these boys."

These boys.

Pressing around her.

Shivering.

A seagull skims the surface of the Rhein with a husky cry and captures a fish.

Andreas nudges Heinz. "My *Oma* comes from Bavaria, too."

Thekla angles her elbows to keep the boys away from her. "I have never asked Sister Josefine for permission to teach in nature."

"In my school you would."

She feels a sudden rage. *Ten years to find this position, and I'm not letting you take it from me.*

*

Gisela scratches her knuckles. Already, she can see herself telling Günther how she walked around the living room with loud steps, calling Bruno's name; and though he'll be annoyed at Bruno for making him late for lunch and possibly late for school, she'll get him to laugh with her—the way only parents will at the quirks of their children—because they both know how Bruno can get with his hiding games, and it will be good to laugh together because, lately, there has not been enough of that in their house.

*

This is what she will do, Thekla decides: speak with Sister Josefine before Herr Stosick can. As soon as she gets her boys to school, she'll ask the principal for a meeting, complain that Herr Stosick—no, she'll refer to him as the principal of the Protestant school—intimidated the Catholic students. The impropriety of it! Maybe she won't complain but rather consult Sister Josefine for advice on how to handle this impropriety. The sister likes giving advice. It'll be one principal against another. One religion against another. If Thekla has to, she'll incite the nuns into a bloody Holy War, wimples flying, rosaries in an uproar.

*

As Gisela lays her hand on the doorknob, she can feel her son inside the wardrobe, smiling, waiting. She wouldn't have done that at his age. Not in the dark. Except for that one summer night she strayed from the bonfire she'd built with her youth group, drifted toward a glow that shimmered through the night and competed with the flames. It wasn't like her to wander off, but the stars were so near it didn't occur to her she was by herself. It was only natural to climb up to that platform high in a tree, toward the Milky Way, which spread above her and above the spires of the trees as if cut into the night; and as she lay on the wooden planks, she was no longer tethered to earth, only to those stars in their wide band that brought the sky closer to her. She wishes Bruno could have seen how, within that whitish light, every possible color existed—yellow and red and green and blue—in uncounted variations. When she heard her friends' voices yelling her name, she didn't answer because she didn't want this to end, this whiteness in the sky and she, only she, part of it. As she breathed slowly to make this last, it occurred to her that she didn't have to go back, that she could let herself be sucked into that whiteness. Her friends walked on, and their shouts grew muffled, into echoes of shouts that could not touch her, echoes of echoes.

*

Herr Stosick is peering into the faces of the boys as if expecting to recognize his son.

"Please, Herr Stosick—" The young teacher keeps her voice polite. "I'm sure you'll find Bruno at home."

She wants him to go away, let her complete this afternoon with her boys, keep them warm and focused. She'll have a race back to school. Already, she can picture Wolfgang leaning forward, the first to sprint.

"How did you lose him?" Herr Stosick demands.

"He didn't come with us," Thekla says.

"What?"

"Gisela kept him home."

"No, she didn't."

"He wasn't feeling well. His face and hands were cold. She must have taken him to Frau Doktor Rosen."

That's when he starts away from her toward the dike.

*

Gisela smiles to herself as she imagines Bruno raising his face toward the scent of the *Himmel und Erde* she's prepared the way he likes it, no salt, so that the sweetness of the apples overwhelms the potatoes. Her Bruno adores— Her hands are itching. Fingertips to knuckles. She rubs them, hard. Her Bruno adores sweets, and it's for him that she will boil down the first raspberries next summer into syrup that he'll dribble on his rice pudding to make it last.

*

The boys keep in one tight formation around their teacher until she manages to break from them and rush after Bruno's father. Then they huddle, think of staying behind, to climb on the jetties, aim pebbles for the current that rushes past them toward the left, and determine who can skip the farthest.

Fräulein Jansen has shown them the Rhein on the map of the world, no more than a squiggle; but on the map of Germany, they've followed their river past Duisburg and Xanten to the Dutch border, studying its geology and history. "It doesn't stop at the border, of course," Fräulein said as she drew the rest of the Rhein on the chalkboard, adding Dutch towns along its banks, Rijnwaarden and Zevenaar and Rotterdam, until the Rhein spilled itself into the Nordsee.

Here, by the river, they won't have to be careful not to break windows or hit people and animals who might stray. But staying behind would mean letting Fräulein chase after Bruno's father alone. She's theirs to protect. That's why the boys keep up with her. Easy. Because it's at the slow pace of Bruno's father. While he steps around horse droppings, the boys leap across. He has to slow down as he climbs the dike with the vast sky above him. It would take no effort to pass him, trip him, close around him once he's on the ground.

In the stubbly fields hang the tattered clothes of leftover scarecrows. At the Braunmeiers' farm, the boys try to pester the white goat by clapping their hands, but the goat perches on its favorite tree stump in the middle of the meadow like a statue, like the king of all the cows that clump together at a distance.

When the boys pass the slaughterhouse and head into the heart of their village, their formation disperses and tightens—with their rivalry, with their bonding against one enemy: Bruno's father—a precursor to what they will experience in the next war, when they'll belong to units that will move as one, every man obliged to do his share of what must be done. Because not to would saddle your comrade with what's yours to finish.

*

The itching races from Gisela's wrists up her arms. She rotates them against the sides of her dress, pictures herself telling Günther how she can feel Bruno on the other side of the door, holding his breath so she won't hear him, eager to jump out and shout the instant she yanks the door open—"I thought you'd never find me, *Mutti*!"—but she won't tell Günther about the crazy thoughts that overtake her the instant she pulls at the door—jammed, it's jammed—pulls again though something primeval and terrible is jabbering inside her *don't look don't lookdon'tlookdon't—*

1914

Chapter 29

WHEN HIS YOUNGEST son was nine, Wilhelm Jansen was sent away to fight in the Great War. But after just a few months he was brought back to his family—on a stretcher on a train—though his skin was unbroken except for one nick on his chin where he'd cut himself eating goat cheese from the blade of his knife. From then on, the dark waves were there nearly all the time.

Frau Doktor Rosen said something was broken inside the toymaker's mind.

Herr Pastor Schüler said it was his soul.

Until the trenches of war, Wilhelm had managed to put together the broken pieces of himself, heroically, again and again; but in the trenches, all those pieces collided and flew apart.

*

Other soldiers, too, returned early, broken from the battlefields and the blinding rush toward oblivion. They'd lie on their beds all day. Or you'd see them on chairs by their windows. War had decimated the threshold between them and the shadows. Yet, you couldn't tell they were injured. That's why they were worse off than soldiers whose injuries were evident—the loss of an arm, say, or of a leg—because you could acknowledge those soldiers' loss and heroism by carving a wooden limb, say, or a crutch; or by helping with chores they could no longer do.

This brokenness was more crippling than blindness or scarred lungs from the nerve gas that had overtaken many as they ran from it. Escape was your first impulse when that green, stinking cloud fanned toward you, and you'd forget what you'd been taught in training, to stop and piss on your handkerchief or sleeve and press the wet fabric over your face to counteract the gas.

The only injuries worse than the brokenness were the injuries of soldiers who were kept out of sight in faraway infirmaries because their wounds made them too grotesque to live among others.

*

Some men would stop by the pay-library because Leo Montag understood what it was like to have fought in the Great War and come home damaged. The circle of steel where his kneecap used to be brought him closer to the men, as if an angel in high flight—that's what he'd looked like before the war as a gymnast levitating above the parallel bars—had crashed to earth. His limp was proof that he was here to stay, to listen.

In Leo Montag's eyes, men could see the places that had shaped their own souls. They had no idea that quite a few of the women in town would have traded their men for Leo, who was gentle and tragic and more manly, somehow, than the most able-bodied men who could still carry great weights and run without limping.

*

To his neighbors, Wilhelm Jansen seemed shut away inside a sadness deeper than caves. They didn't understand the swiftness of bliss beneath his inertia, bliss when he made love to his wife or peered at the faces of his children. For a while, he returned to the toy factory. Children no longer wanted lambs or fairy-tale blocks—they wanted to play with soldiers. But the soldiers he carved, bright yellow or green uniforms, were not at all like soldiers in the real war where the only bright color was that of blood before it dulled.

Alexander Sturm believed in providing the wounded with a place where they could do work that satisfied them, and though Wilhelm missed days, he kept him on because Wilhelm was the most gifted carver he'd ever hired, and because they both recognized that making toys was serious business. He hired two other toymakers who'd come back early from battle, lungs damaged by gas; he set up a bed and reminded them to take turns resting. Together, the three men completed the tasks of one.

Wilhelm's sons helped by bringing their earnings—given to them in food or coins—to their mother. From an early age, they were good workers, eager for the smallest jobs, and the old women of Burgdorf approved of their industriousness. But they did not approve of how the Jansen girl was pampered. It set her above her brothers, the women gossiped, and it was wrong of Almut Jansen to let the daughter have the best, the first, not used by anyone before her. Girls' things, they couldn't be passed down to her brothers once she outgrew them, except for boots and one cornflower-blue sweater that Elmar, and then Dietrich, had worn down to the skin of their elbows, and that Almut had darned countless times until there were no more threads left to anchor her weave of darning.

*

Whenever Wilhelm's hours outside the shadows grew longer than the hours inside, he dared hope that, in time, he'd forget the passage to there altogether. Easier, then, to study his hands than the faces of his children, who would grow up with the fear that they'd inherit his craziness, especially his youngest son, Dietrich, moody and athletic, who would become a priest, while Elmar, pious and delicate, the son his teachers predicted would become a priest, would work for the potato man, Herr Weinhart, making deliveries though he'd hate the cloud of old potato dust that would billow around him whenever he'd empty sacks of new potatoes into the tops of his customers' bins.

Tuesday, February 27, 1934

Chapter 30

THE SHRIEKING COMES at the boys as they turn the corner to Bruno's street, a shrieking that's as much sound as motion as it whirls toward them like sand and becomes Bruno's mother whirling toward them, all of one color, the color of sand—hair lips clothes—and already Bruno's father is running into the sand, staggering as if bracing against a fierce wind.

Shrieking. The sand. Shrieking at Bruno's father. " . . . he did it!"

"What are you—"

" . . . then I found him! Oh God!"

The shrieking irritates the boys the way sand will when it gets into your eyes, your nostrils, and already their irritation is shifting to Bruno. They'll get him for this. Get him for wrecking their learning excursion. They could still be by the river climbing willows and watching the yellow ferry cross to their side. They could be getting ready for a race, leaning forward, ready to sprint, and then their legs flashing. Of course Wolfgang would win, but they'd raise him high into the air, only pretend to drop him, making the teacher laugh, even Eckart.

*

Bruno's mother is the sand shrieking: "Dead . . . he's dead!"

Fräulein Jansen covers her lips with both hands.

"No!" Bruno's father howls.

They draw closer, the boys, listen to the sand shrieking till they can picture Bruno with the top button of his uniform open so the rope fits around his neck, can hear Bruno shrieking while the rope cuts off his breath—

But it's still his mother doing all the shrieking: " . . . if I had opened the living room door all the way, I would have seen the chess books and sets on the floor. I would have been early enough to stop him . . ."

The teacher wants to shield her boys from hearing, wants to shield herself, and she spans her arms, pulls her boys close, as many as she can touch, even if it's just with the ends of her fingers.

" . . . the sound I heard when I came back from looking for him at school must have been Bruno in the chess wardrobe, getting the rope ready to . . ."

They crowd against the teacher, the boys, oddly excited because Bruno's death makes them different, makes them important. Only this morning they fretted about the anniversary of the Reichstag fire; but now they know someone their age who has died, who has done it to himself, the dying.

" . . . while I was at his school, he must have removed the books and chess sets to make room for himself in there so . . ."

If only I'd walked Bruno home, the teacher thinks. If only I'd handed him over to his mother.

First to arrive is the bakery truck. Then the police. Then Trudi Montag from the pay-library. How did she get here so quickly on her short legs? the boys wonder. She's always kind to them, but they've been warned to keep family matters from her because she can tell just by looking at you—*but how can that be?*—what you don't want her to know. Once she has your secret, she makes it bigger by carrying it from door to door, bartering it for other secrets.

*

All rain has ceased, but the air is drenched with the memory of water. Only one ribbon of snow lies along the edge of Bruno's sidewalk, a ribbon the boys are not allowed to cross. While Bruno is on the other side of that ribbon. Inside his house. Inside the wardrobe.

But the police can cross.

And Bruno's parents.

But only Bruno's mother crosses, her fingers scratching up and down her arms. Scratching.

Bruno's father does not cross into his house. Bruno's father is howling. *Feigling*—coward, the boys think.

Because they would go inside. And look. And remember. Death has been glorious in poems about heroes, but this death here is different because Bruno is no hero, and Bruno's father is a *Feigling.*

*

The wingbeats of pigeons as they land above on the windowsill of the teacher's apartment. Her face is wet from crying. She'll miss the sound of Bruno's voice in the mornings, his visits to her. She can't live here anymore. The Stosicks wouldn't want her to. She hates herself for that selfishness. Her loss is nothing compared to that of his parents. Still—

And what if Sister Josefine dismisses her for not asking permission?

Did you ever ask permission, Fräulein Siderova, before you took us on a learning excursion?

Here she's doing it again, worrying about herself when it is all about Bruno's death.

"It's always about you," Dietrich used to say. She thought it was because of his envy. Having while he and Elmar didn't: books and clothes and education and a good bicycle. Dietrich had facial hair early on, an amazing mustache when he was just seventeen and entered the seminary. "You're doing it again," he would tell Thekla if he were here. "Hogging. Hogging even grief." Dietrich must be hell on his parishioners, especially in the confessional. For his first post as assistant pastor, he finessed an assignment to Nordstrand though he wasn't supposed to ask, just obey his superiors and go where he was sent. *It's always about you, Dietrich.*

*

Herr Stosick is still howling. To leave that greedy self of hers—greedy, Frau Abramowitz called her—and to make him stop this disgusting wet noise, Thekla steps toward him, touches his arm; but he startles her by flinging himself against her, howling, so massive and dense that his body feels like one block drumming against her, one block that cannot delegate different tasks to arms and legs because it's moving as one, all belly, strong belly, muscles pounding against her, against her breasts, disturbing her, arousing her—

I've never been with a heavy man. Never expected that this mass of flesh in my arms would arouse me. She struggles to free herself from this odd embrace, but he holds on as though he had a right to her, and she suddenly knows he's been getting part of her rent from Herr Abramowitz, knows it in a way so apparent it's impossible not to know once you consider it. Her mother must have heard from Herr Abramowitz about the apartment, and they must have arranged it all before Thekla went to look at it.

So that's why Herr Stosick avoided her comment about the low rent. Instead he distracted her with flattery. An honor to have her live in his house. *Honor.* His colleague, he called her. And her silly pride at being able to afford her own place. While all along Herr Abramowitz was paying for her. *Being poor but looking rich.* And again, that shame at having more than others. While Herr Stosick is howling, clinging to her. *But I didn't do anything wrong to get his apartment. I—*

*

Cooking smells from the Stosicks' kitchen. *Himmel und Erde.* Whenever Thekla's mother cooks—

How can I think of food?

—Himmel und Erde, the smell is not this sweet because she mashes more potatoes than apples. Potatoes are free for Thekla's family. Elmar smuggles them in, smooth contraband, so that *Mutti* doesn't have to touch wrinkled potatoes and—

What did I already know when I drew Herr Abramowitz into my Noah's ark? Thekla pushes it away, has to, but it reasserts itself, and she knows it will be there from this instant forward, knows it by her immeasurable sorrow for *Vati. Nonsense, it's all nonsense.* Of course *Vati* is her father; and yet, Herr Abramowitz is forever carrying food and toys and clothes into the kitchen, where *Vati* sits without voice, without motion, sits forever in his shiny-bare Sunday suit as close to the stove as he can without burning himself, hands on his thighs like something broken as he stares at the floor between his black shoes.

Are Herr Abramowitz and *Mutti* still lovers? He provided for Thekla like a father, but not for her brothers, though he could have paid for their education, too. Instead he set her apart from Elmar and Dietrich. Set them against her. Dietrich, no more than four years old, screaming: "You stay away from *Vati*. He's mine."

What did I already know? Because if Herr Abramowitz is, if he really is my father—

A jolt of fear. *And what will happen to me then?* No—

Because what if thinking comes from wishing and makes it so? What then? What if I want his courage and strength instead of Wilhelm's shadows? What if that's all?

How much do the Stosicks know? The townspeople? No proof.

I don't have to tell anyone.

No proof at all.

*

Her boys are scowling at Bruno's father. If there had to be a man for their teacher, they'd want someone handsome. He's clinging to her so hard that she feels his suspenders through his jacket.

"You should be with your wife." She wedges her palms against his chest.

But his arms only tighten around her.

"And I should be with my students."

He doesn't budge. Not when Frau Doktor Rosen and Herr Pastor Schüler are rushed into his house. Not when Trudi Montag tugs at his elbow and asks what she can do to help him. Others are arriving as if catastrophe had pulled them here. As they all wait, the wet air hangs around them, fills them.

"What can we do?"

"How did it happen?"

Wind rustles the dry *Hortensie*—hydrangea against the brick wall. Winter lace in his winter garden. It was blooming when Thekla rented her apartment. Already, a splinter of waning moon is rushing them past Bruno's death, toward the memory of his death, less acute with each day, each year, as all of them hurdle toward their own deaths.

Mine, too.

My death, too.

Chapter 31

"SHE WOULD HAVE BEEN GOOD as the mother of a dozen children."

"It would have given her some spare children."

"She doesn't know how to be alone."

By the edge of the house, a tangle of women whisper how difficult it was for Gisela to conceive and carry a child to term, how she'll be alone once again and forever, alone in the way you can't be if you have a child who's always one heartbeat from yours, *one heartbeat,* until one of the hearts stops beating, yours or your child's, and if it is your child's heart—*out of sequence, not right, not thinkable*—your heart may as well stop, too.

Those women who've lost a child know that.

A child lost soon after birth.

Or in its early years: death from influenza . . . falling from a tractor.

A grown daughter lost to childbirth.

A grown son—half grown, really—lost to the Great War. Some women held still for ceremonies that honored them for being mothers of heroes, rewarded them for not raging publicly at their sons' deaths but waiting with that rage till they could crawl back into the barren of their lives. Other women took solace from the ceremonies because it was tempting to believe their sons had been felled by the enemy while protecting the homeland. These women carried the weight of that glory, rather than the weight of their sorrow. Still, always, always, there were those mothers who would not submit to the ceremonies; who carried their sorrow and rage in the blaze of their faces, their bodies; who'd rather spurn honor than pretend it replaced their sons.

*

Herr Stosick, pressing against Thekla. And her body— Pressing back? She feels sick with guilt and disgust. He has lost his son, has come to her for comfort, and all she offers him is her twisted lust. The men she's been with are like Emil. Muscular. Slender—

And there he is, Emil, as if she had evoked him. With him is Leo Montag. "Günther," they say and take Herr Stosick by the shoulders. "Günther—"

He shakes his head as if rising from a daze, and it takes the strength of both men to pry him away from Thekla.

An icy draft against the front of her coat where the heat of his body was before.

While Leo Montag leads Günther Stosick into the house, Emil stays with Thekla, nudges her lips with a cigarette. But they stay closed. He takes off his right glove, strokes her lips with his index finger till she opens them.

As he strikes a match, she murmurs, "Van der Lubbe had matches on him when they caught him."

Normally Emil would tell her that was not enough evidence. But he doesn't.

So she says it: "Not enough evidence."

He studies her. Nods.

"Still . . . they blamed him."

One arm around her back, he steadies her.

How could I have ever thought of letting him go?

Otto is glaring at his teacher. She has gone from one man's arms into another's, and Otto doesn't like it one bit. He longs to betray her—but just for that instant, because already she's walking away from the man, toward Otto and the other boys.

*

The shame of their excitement has made them jumpy because from now on they'll be the boys who knew Bruno before he made himself dead. Bruno, who'll stay forever the age they are today. While they'll grow up past where he stopped it for himself, the growing up and the growing beyond.

What can I possibly do to calm them?

And then Thekla knows. Schiller's *"Der Taucher"*—"The Diver." No need to wait with the poem till tomorrow. She motions her boys closer, keeps her voice low as she recites the first stanza:

> *"Wer wagt es, Rittersmann oder Knapp,*
> *Zu tauchen in diesen Schlund?*
> *Einen golden Becher werf ich hinab,*
> *Verschlungen schon hat ihn der schwarze Mund.*
> *Wer mir den Becher kann wieder zeigen,*
> *Er mag ihn behalten, er ist sein eigen."*

The boys are holding their breath for the young diver who, like many of them, is both *sanft und keck*—mild and audacious, as he takes the reckless king's challenge and leaps into the churning waters to retrieve the golden cup.

"Repeat after me," their teacher says.

Her boys huddle, repeat her words: the first stanza, the next, and the ones after that. Their voices grow hopeful when the diver's pale arm emerges from the sea with his prize.

"The end," the teacher says.

The boys don't suspect that she's ending the poem before Schiller did.

She doesn't want to frighten them with the king's *grausame Spiel*—cruel game as he goads the diver to take the second leap into the rough waters that will crush him against the cliff. The poem isn't even about courage that's asked of you by fate. No, what the mad king asks for is loyalty to him during chaos of his making.

She feels guilty for bending Schiller to fit what her boys need. She'll owe Schiller—and her boys—these missing stanzas. Next week.

Or next month. For now, let them believe that the young page gets to keep the golden cup. Let them believe he gets the princess and the fairy-tale ending: living *vergnügt bis an ihr Ende*—joyously until their end.

*

Members of the chess club are still arriving—not to play chess but to offer their stunned condolence through their presence. Some leave right away, reluctant to be seen with the Stosicks, who forced their son to quit the Hitler-Jugend and will likely be blamed for his death.

But those who stay cluster outside the house in the membrane of their freezing breaths and cigarette smoke, voiceless at this child's willful death, the only sound their feet scuffing the frozen ground. They would never admit that already they feel more intelligent, freed to compete against one another from now on, not against this strange and brilliant boy, who made them feel slow and forgetful as if all the chess games they'd studied and analyzed for decades were leaking from their minds. They will come to remember that they were the dead boy's mentors, that his certainty with chess moves was the result of what they'd taught him, a certainty that was appropriate in unnerving out-of-town opponents but disrespectful when used against his mentors.

Finally, one speaks: "Supposed to get even colder."

Then another: "Have they cut the boy down?"

"You can't wash in frozen water, my *Mutter* used to say."

"Why would they leave him hanging like—"

"This will cost Günther . . . taking his boy out of the Hitler-Jugend—"

"They'll have to use pickaxes on the earth."

"To open it for the body."

Just four hours from now, the people of Burgdorf will be aware that—exactly one year ago—the Reichstag burned. Once tonight passes, most will feel safe once more because the Führer's foresight and decisiveness prevented it from happening again.

But some will recognize the queasy weight of premonition having come into being. They all feared that the catastrophe would repeat itself in its familiar shape: fire. Instead the catastrophe destroyed one of their children.

*

"When you get home," the teacher tells her boys, "I want you to think about Schiller's poem and draw a picture of the diver." It feels odd to assign them homework. But not to would leave them idle, open to fear. She wants the assignment to occupy the space in their minds where Bruno's death is.

"Please, bring your drawing to class tomorrow," she reminds them.

Once again, she recites the poem from the beginning, but as her boys repeat after her, their chorus gets smaller because some parents are arriving, taking their sons home. Other parents stay. When Thekla has only three students left—Eckart and Heinz and

Andreas—she takes them home in the dusk though they're accustomed to walking back and forth to school alone.

Only then does she run toward Fräulein Siderova's apartment on Schlosserstrasse.

1933

May 10–12

Chapter 32

THE SECOND WEDNESDAY of May 1933 a *Fackelzug*—torch parade marched past Fräulein Siderova's window. Songs and uniforms. Students wheeling handcarts full of books. Quickly, Fräulein switched on her *Volksempfänger*. A broadcast from Berlin. And its echo—

—an echo that filled the streets and seemed to come from the Burgdorf market square, condemning writers for lying, exploiting the German language to write *undeutsche Gedanken*—un-German thoughts and thereby betraying the German youth. From now on forward, the German youth would be called upon to ensure that German literature would be noble and clean.

*

Thekla pressed herself against the wet stone wall of the Rathaus. In the market square, rain and smoke thickened the air so that it flickered like a stage curtain made from strips of gauze to keep people from seeing clearly. As they passed through that flicker, their movements were jerky, the way you'd see them in a lightning storm if they were to run for shelter. Except they were not fleeing; they were rushing toward the pyre in the middle of the square, children and women and men, hurling books through the arc of smoke into the flames, shouting *Feuersprüche*—fire recitations, as if part of a staged performance with a huge cast, like Wagner's *Meistersinger* when the cobbler sings about watching out for the evil tricks that threaten the German Volk and Reich.

*

Twice, Fräulein Siderova made sure her door was locked. A nimbus of fire shivered from the direction of the square. Then shouts, a chorus of *Feuersprüche*.

"*Gegen Klassenkampf und Materialismus*—against class-struggle and materialism . . . *Ich übergebe der Flamme die Schriften von Karl Marx*—I relegate to the flame the writings of Karl Marx . . . ."

"*Gegen seelenzerfasernde Überschätzung des Trieblebens*—Against soul-shattering exaggeration of the sex life . . . *Ich übergebe der Flamme die Schriften von Sigmund Freud*—I relegate to the flame the writings of Sigmund Freud!"

For weeks now, Fräulein Siderova's school had become a drop-off center for *undeutsche Bücher*—un-German books, and schoolchildren had been ransacking classrooms, stacking books in the corridor. Some children brought in books they'd located under their grandparents' beds or behind their parents' bookshelves. Townspeople arrived to relinquish *undeutsche Bücher*: dirty books, books that belonged to the past. In the corridor, students could no longer run without toppling over these stacks that grew taller against the walls and around the statue of the giant, St. Christopher, until the little Jesus who sat on the saint's shoulder seemed to float on a sea of books.

*

Thekla hoped Fräulein Siderova couldn't hear the loudspeakers set up in the square, Goebbels's voice from Berlin urging all Germans to prove their courage by burning *undeutsche Bücher*. Seventy-one writers on the blacklist! Arthur Schnitzler and Anna Seghers and Marcel Proust and Upton Sinclair and Theodor Wolff and Georg Bernhard and Erich Maria Remarque . . .

"*Gegen literarischen Verrat am Soldaten des Weltkrieges, für Erziehung des Volkes Im Geist der Wahrhaftigkeit*—Against the literary betrayal of soldiers in the Great War, for the education of the Volk in the spirit of truth . . . *Ich übergebe der Flamme die Schriften von Erich Maria Remarque*—I relegate to the flame the writings of Erich Maria Remarque. . . ."

How could Remarque's *Im Westen nichts Neues*—*All Quiet on the Western Front* suddenly be unpatriotic? A novel that had been praised and read by over a million? Thekla knew if she asked that aloud, she might be accused of strengthening the enemy, perhaps even arrested like Herr Zimmer, who was trying to prevent two of his students from emptying a handcart of books into the fire.

*

"Against decadence and moral collapse . . . I relegate to the flame the writings of Heinrich Mann . . . of Erich Kästner . . ."

Fräulein Siderova thought of Jews all over Germany, curved toward their radios behind locked doors, while the savage crowds shouted about cleansing literature, and she wondered if they, too, were thinking how two crucial changes in their country were brought about by fire.

"*Neues Leben, neues Schrifttum, neuer Glaube blühe aus den Ruinen*—new life, new writing, new belief shall blossom from the ruins."

Couldn't they hear how, in their enthusiasm to cleanse, they contaminated language?

On the radio a pause, then crackling and an interview with a professor of literature who stated it was better to burn too many books than to miss a single one. This from a professor of literature? He surely had to know Heine's words "*Dort, wo man Bücher verbrennt, verbrennt man am Ende auch Menschen*—where they burn books, they will ultimately also burn people."

*

Flames tore into the spines of the books, into their soft centers. People were taking off their hats and kerchiefs. Their heads were bare as they sang: "*Nun danket alle Gott*—now let us all thank God."

After that: *"Sieg Heil."* Three times.

A haze shivered around the flames and smoke, like a second breath, and Thekla wondered if standing here meant she was one of these people. Sick with fear, she tried to step away but was trapped between the crowd and the Rathaus. Until now, she had taken for granted that she had moral courage, but suddenly she didn't know if it was possible to defer moral courage, conserve it, and if it would still be there for her, or if each moment like this would take her into another silent agreement, and another yet, until she'd find herself agreeing to what she'd never imagined, and she would have to adjust what she believed about herself.

Chapter 33

SOME BOOKS WERE still smoldering at dawn, but most had disintegrated to ashes when the cleaning crews shoveled them into wheelbarrows, swept the market square, and hauled away the debris.

Yet, the charred remains got tracked throughout the village, got inside your houses, and soiled your floors even if you hadn't been near the pyre. As the smell of wet ashes seeped through your closed windows and doors, it settled in your bedding, your clothing, your wardrobes. The affront of that smell—flat and nasty—made you want to spit. You were sure you'd never get used to it; and yet despite your ceaseless scrubbing and airing, it would become part of your own smell, in your breath, on your skin, increasingly familiar.

*

When Fräulein Siderova arrived at the Catholic school, the corridors were slick with black mud that children and teachers were dragging in on their soles though Sister Mäuschen reminded them to wipe their feet. She'd brought out every floor mat she'd found in the school and in the convent, but already these, too, were turning soggy, black.

Fräulein Siderova didn't let her students see how shaken she was. She steadied herself by following her lesson plan on the Trojan War. Last week they'd started by sketching the colossal draft horse behind the brewery. When they'd voted on which sketch to use for their papier-mâché sculpture of the Trojan horse, Markus Bachmann's had won. The boys had brought in newspapers and fabric scraps and horsehair and bits of fur. Together, they'd built a magnificent horse with a trapdoor in the underside of its belly.

For today, they'd brought toy soldiers, miniature German soldiers with helmets that the boys stashed inside the horse's belly, though Bruno objected that they were not authentic.

"We don't have any Greek soldiers," Richard said.

"Once they're inside, you won't see them," Andreas said.

"But I'll know," Bruno said.

Fräulein Siderova praised the boys when they read their assignment aloud, one paragraph told in the voice of their favorite character from the passages she'd read to them in the *Iliad*. Nearly half of the boys chose Achilles, the brave and handsome Greek hero; three were Paris, also brave and handsome, but a Trojan hero. Two each were Ajax, the tallest warrior, and Homer, who'd written it all down. One Zeus. One Poseidon.

For Sonja Siderova it had always been Cassandra, fascinating and influential. Cassandra, blessed by Apollo to see into the future. But when she resisted his courtship, Apollo revenged himself with the curse that no one would give credence to her prophesies.

*

That afternoon, the principal of the Catholic school knocked on the door of the house where Thekla lived with her parents. "Can you start teaching tomorrow?" she asked.

"Tomorrow?" Thekla stopped breathing.

One day's notice to start the work she'd been longing for? The honor of that. While countless others were still waiting. All those years Fräulein Siderova had encouraged her to believe she would find a position. She'd reminded her principal that Thekla Jansen was her best student ever, and would be an inspiring teacher. And now Sister Josefine was here as though Fräulein Siderova had sent her, with her wide, wide shoulders and trim waist, the body of a horseback rider that her nun's habit couldn't conceal.

"Would you like to come inside?" Thekla asked.

"No."

The wet smell of ashes spun around Sister Josefine, sealed her and Thekla in that moment of standing outside the door.

"Yes," Thekla said and already pictured herself telling Fräulein Siderova . . . the joy in her kind face.

"Please," Thekla said.

"Tomorrow," Thekla said.

"Fourth grade," Sister Josefine said,

"But that's Fräulein Siderova's class!" Thekla cried out. She was ready to tell Sister Josefine she couldn't take the class from her teacher. Started to say, "Please, don't—"

But she stopped herself. At least they hadn't arrested Fräulein Siderova like Herr Zimmer, who'd also lost his teaching job at the Protestant school. But Herr Zimmer was a Jew *and* a communist. While Fräulein Siderova was more Catholic than Jewish. A child when she left Russia. Certainly no reason to be considered a communist.

"Tomorrow," Thekla told Sister Josefine before she could stop herself, in her belly that familiar queasiness of doing something wrong. Knowing she was doing something wrong and still doing it. "I'll be at school tomorrow."

The instant Sister Josefine left with that long stride of hers—*you know how she walks, Fräulein Siderova, flaunting her muscles through the cloth of her habit*—Thekla started toward Fräulein Siderova's house to warn her.

Except I did not walk that far. Only up to the corner. Still, she could see herself running to Schlosserstrasse and up the stairs to Fräulein Siderova's apartment. But then it occurred to her how awkward it would be if Sister Josefine were to find her there. She couldn't jeopardize the teaching position. *For both of us.* Better to wait a few hours. Once Sister Josefine had told Fräulein Siderova, Thekla would return, console her teacher, assure her that she'd do whatever she could to bring her back to school.

She went home. Wrote her lesson plan for Fräulein Siderova's students. It was evening then, too late for a proper visit, and she promised herself she'd go the following afternoon.

Chapter 34

BUT IN THE MORNING Fräulein Siderova walked into the teachers' lounge, elegant and swift as always, while Thekla was still unbuttoning her camel hair coat. She wanted to hide, but Fräulein Siderova grasped her hands, face so radiant that Thekla thought she had to be the most forgiving person on earth.

"Does this mean they finally hired you, Thekla?"

That's when I knew you hadn't been told. And I felt like a Judas.

"Now we'll be colleagues." Fräulein Siderova bent toward her. "I'm ecstatic . . . for you and for me."

Thekla tried to speak.

"Which grade will you be teaching?"

Thekla's throat felt raw. "Fourth."

Fräulein Siderova hooked two fingertips across the silver rims of her spectacles. Closed her eyes. "I see," she whispered. As if she could. *See.* See how her tolerance for the fear of others would change until she'd feel brittle, forlorn when she'd read to the dying;

how she would receive fewer requests and how people would speculate that fear was clotting inside her; how they'd speak to the priest about their concerns, but not to her because they'd be embarrassed to draw her into their midst while trying to avoid her; how they'd whisper that she wanted to keep herself separate from them because certain family treasures came into her possession; how the pharmacist would accuse her openly of having his mother's vase, and how she'd remind him that his mother gave it to her the night she died, and how he'd tell her she must have done something to make his mother give her the vase.

"I left the vase with the priest," Fräulein Siderova said.

"Which vase?" Thekla asked.

"For the pharmacist."

"I— I didn't ask Sister Josefine for your position."

"Of course you didn't ask." As Fräulein Siderova slid off her spectacles, they dropped to the floor. Tiny veins on her smooth eyelids, veins barely raised from the translucent skin.

To retrieve them, Thekla crouched by the long library table. One of its legs was smaller than the others, the wood lighter, as though it had been replaced. Why hadn't she noticed before? It seemed an important question, a question to wrap her soul around.

"I've always taught girls," Fräulein Siderova was saying. "When Sister Josefine gave me a class of boys this spring, I should have known. . . ."

Thekla felt odd to be kneeling at her feet. Specks of ashes. Dustings of ashes. When she handed up the spectacles, Fräulein Siderova's fingers didn't close around them.

"I'm sorry." Carefully, Thekla folded the spectacles. Slipped them into the pocket of Fräulein Siderova's silk jacket.

"Still . . . ," Fräulein Siderova said. "Still . . . better you than one of them."

One of them? Do you know how that cut through me? "I don't even think of you as Jewish," Thekla said.

Fräulein Siderova's chin puckered, deepening that oblong dimple.

"You pray at St. Martin's," Thekla said. "You sing in the church choir. I'll tell Sister Josefine about the Christmas angels you make with your students."

Couldn't you feel how I wanted to help you? Just as you had helped me, inviting me into the classroom to get teaching experience.

Suddenly, Thekla knew what she had to do to save the position for Fräulein Siderova. "I'll teach your class till you come back," she promised, "only till then."

Tuesday, February 27, 1934

Chapter 35

LAMPLIGHT BEHIND the bay window at Schlosserstrasse 78.

In the stairway the familiar mint smell that blots all other smells.

When Fräulein Siderova opens the door—bedsheets in her arms, used sheets in a bundle—Thekla's childhood love for her teacher rushes at her so strongly that she doesn't know how she survived without that love.

"I must tell you—"

But Fräulein Siderova turns from her, carries the sheets into the bathroom.

Grateful she didn't close the door, Thekla runs after her, slips around her to open the hamper. Pulse in her throat so high she can't say another word, she waits for Fräulein Siderova to look at her, but her teacher simply drops the sheets inside the hamper, gets fresh sheets from the shelves, and takes them to the spare room.

Lined up under the edge of the bed are two slippers. The mattress is bare. *Have you been expecting me?* Thekla feels disoriented. *Are you getting the bed ready for me? How do you know I can no longer live at the Stosicks'?* She could imagine living here with Fräulein Siderova, walk to school just as her teacher used to. *Selfish—* Selfish for not thinking about Bruno every second. Selfish for her relief that she no longer has to have that conversation with the Stosicks about Bruno climbing from his window at night. She forces herself to imagine him beneath the ground. But not yet. For now, he is still inside his house. *So light in my arms when I hold him at his christening celebration. I'm still at the university, and I have no idea that this long, skinny baby who doesn't cry will be in my first group of students and that he'll take his own life. Bruno—*

How then do you reach into this with both hands, Fräulein Siderova, and change Bruno's fate?

*

"How then—" Thekla breaks off.

How dare I ask this? You believed you could change fate. But what if it was predetermined that Bruno would kill himself when he was ten? And what if it was predetermined that you would set out geraniums for a butterfly? And what if it was predetermined that Almut and Michel would make a child?

Thekla picks up a pillow, shakes it, and inserts it in the pillowcase. Though Fräulein Siderova presses her lips together, she does not object. Together they unfold the bottom sheet and make the bed as they have made beds with others, though never together. Thekla steps around the slippers, large—*men's slippers?*—not of good quality, one heel so worn it slants toward the other.

Once I tell you what happened to Bruno, tell you everything, Fräulein Siderova, will you send me away forever? Or will you say that I did all I could for our boys? Will you tell me to lie down on this ironed sheet, cover me, and tell me to sleep?

"I lost one of your boys," Thekla whispers. "Bruno—he's dead."

Like a blind woman, Sonja Siderova reaches behind herself with both hands, pats the air till her fingers touch the mattress. Awkwardly, she lowers herself.

"I was keeping him safe." Thekla is crying. "I followed him to the rallies at night to keep him safe and . . ."

Sonja has to concentrate, hard, because it's coming at her without sequence: Frau Doktor Rosen rushing inside the Stosicks' house and Bruno saying his father wants the Führer strung up and the boys climbing willows and Frau Stosick finding Bruno inside the chess wardrobe and Herr Stosick tracking Thekla to the Rhein and people outside the Stosicks' house hoping against hope that Bruno is still alive—

"But why?" she moans.

—and Leo Montag leading Herr Stosick into the house and the boys counting barges and the police finding Bruno's pledge to the Führer in his pocket and birds hanging like silver triangles in the sky and—

Sonja Siderova's eyes are so desolate that Thekla fears one more detail will break her. "I'm so sorry. I feel terrible."

"You?" Sonja cries. "Is that why you came here? To be comforted by me?"

"No— I came because I owed you . . . the telling."

"Then tell me. Now."

*

Thekla does: the awful pressure of Herr Stosick's belly against hers and the police saying Bruno wore his uniform in the wardrobe and Gisela Stosick interrupting the teachers' meeting—

But that's before Bruno's death, when his mother interrupts the meeting. It doesn't have to be now. It can be before that. When Bruno runs up the stairs, brings me cake his mother has baked—

But she feels it slipping away, that illusion. "I should be at the

Stosicks' house, helping . . . also if they have questions— But they wouldn't want me there."

Sonja Siderova averts her face.

"When Bruno was crying in school, he must have been planning to kill himself. . . . I should have seen how agitated he was when he said his father wanted the Führer strung up by his balls."

Now Sonja is crying, too. "Bruno didn't know what he was doing."

"I think he knew."

"Children don't always understand the danger of their words."

"He was hoping someone would turn his father in."

"No." Sonja Siderova rubs the bridge of her nose. "He probably just wanted his father out of the way so he could go to his meetings. He never pictured the Gestapo coming to his house and hauling his father away."

"I think he wanted them to take him away. Maybe just for an hour, or a few minutes. But it destroyed him. Oh, God. I should have—" Thekla's head is clogged with Bruno's smell, not the clean sweat smell of her athletic students, but the child-smell of chalk and sleep. *Sleep forever.*

No— Not yet. *I can go back to before your christening, Bruno, long before, when your mother is still a girl, hiding on that platform high in a tree, perhaps dreaming herself a son while we search for her. We won't find her until the sky pales around the stars and fades their outlines.* But Bruno's death pushes itself past the christening and the platform.

"Oh God . . . Bruno—" *I should have carried you home from the rally, snatched you into my arms and run with you from the pomp and the lies and the bonfire.* "What have I been teaching these children? You would have discouraged the boys from joining the Hitler-Jugend. You could see that the parades and uniforms were to get them enthusiastic about being heroes."

"It's what's done to soldiers everywhere. Except they're starting very young here. Child soldiers."

"Jochen Weskopp wants to be a soldier. A hero."

"Children absorb what they are taught. And if the teaching is corrupt—"

"That's why Remarque is banned. Because he wrote about students influenced to romanticize war by—"

"By their teachers, yes. Instead they ended up terrified in the ditches, minds and bodies injured by bullets and nerve gas."

"And Jochen is eight whole years younger than those students. He says after he's a soldier he'll be dead. No fear. No doubt."

"The absence of doubt will turn humans into beasts."

Thekla flinches. How quickly her boys formed a pack.

"You may survive all this, even I . . . but some of our boys already have half their lives behind them. They'll be dead or wounded before they're twenty. *Kanonenfutter*—cannon fodder."

"What can we do?"

"You'll teach. You'll keep our boys alive."

"I wasn't able to keep Bruno alive." *What happens if you're no longer who you believed you were? What do you do with the knowledge of that? And what if who you're becoming goes against what you believed about yourself until you won't remember who you were before?*

"His parents weren't able to keep him alive. I wasn't able to keep him alive. No one—"

"But he came to me."

*

"*Bitte noch etwas Suppe*—please, some more soup." A man's voice. From the kitchen.

Sonja Siderova stands up. "No one in this town was able to keep Bruno alive. Listen to me—" Her wide mouth trembles. "What you can do is show our students other directions . . . especially those students you can't keep from joining."

Thekla follows her to the door, down the hallway past the photos of Fräulein Siderova surrounded by her students, one for each year she has taught. Twenty-nine.

At her kitchen table, a man—not refined—sits with his elbows next to an empty bowl, faint rims of dirt under his fingernails. When Sonja Siderova introduces him as her boarder, Thekla remembers what Fräulein Buttgereit told her. *Not for me then, the bed, the room. How foolish of me. But where will I sleep tonight?*

He's a night-watchman at a bank, Fräulein Siderova says. Definitely not the artist Thekla would have liked to imagine living with her teacher, who will soon paint another portrait of her on another ship, to safety, perhaps.

After the boarder eats his second bowl of soup, he stands up, a stocky man who takes small steps toward the coatrack. How fast could he run if someone were to rob the bank? When he pulls his woolen hat over his forehead, he looks like a bank robber. A slow bank robber. That kind of observation would make Emil laugh. She'll have to tell Emil— *How can I think of laughing when Bruno is dead?*

*

The boarder shrugs into his gray coat, leaves for his job, and Sonja Siderova washes his bowl, his spoon. When Thekla offers to dry, Sonja shakes her head.

"I'm going to take my bath now," she says.

"I'll get the tub ready for you."

"I can do that for myself."

"No need to." Quickly, before Sonja Siderova can tell her to go home, Thekla heads for the bathroom and bends to put in the plug.

"You don't have to do this."

Thekla opens the faucets.

"I don't want to keep you," Sonja says, though just a moment ago, it seemed she might be ready to lift one foot and step across the curved rim into the water.

What Thekla needs is a question to hook her teacher in, a question that will allow her to stay here, and then she has it, has always had it, and it makes her sweat. Because it's more than a hook. Because it's a truth she doesn't want but must have for herself. "Michel Abramowitz— Is he my father?"

Chapter 36

SONJA SIDEROVA DOESN'T HESITATE. "Yes, he is."

Thekla is stunned. Can it really be that easy, finding out for sure? *His hands around an open book. The tracks of his comb in his thick hair.* "What if I had asked you about him last year?"

"I don't know."

"Or when I was a girl? Would you have told me then?"

"Not then."

"Did you tell me to get back at me?" Instantly, Thekla feels ashamed.

Steam rises in the narrow bathroom, fills the lines in Sonja Siderova's face until she looks like the teacher Thekla adored as a girl.

Thekla blinks.

"Get back at you for what?" Fräulein Siderova asks.

"For letting Sister Josefine give me your class."

"Oh, Thekla."

"That's why you're telling me I'm Jewish." Saying it aloud sets off a fear that makes Thekla dizzy. *What will happen to me? No proof. No proof at all. Still, if he is my father— And he is. Is.*

Sonja Siderova motions toward the bathroom door. "I can do the rest by myself." She opens the top button of her blouse.

"One more question? Please?"

"I will take *my* bath now." Sonja opens the next button. "I will take off *my* clothes and take *my* own bath." She removes her silver-rimmed spectacles, folds them, and lays them on the ledge of the tub. Opens another button.

*

Thekla backs away. In the hallway she waits, forehead against the closed bathroom door. Staying feels improper. But she can't bear leaving, now that she is finally near her teacher again. Briefly, it flies at her, the joy at that. *I'll invite you to my classroom, Fräulein Siderova—* But her fantasy doesn't move forward, and she can no longer hide inside plans and manners. *Soon, I'll invite you to my—*

Steam curls from beneath the door, beads on her watch. Splashing— Fräulein Siderova must be lowering herself into the tub.

"If you want more hot or cold water, you can turn the faucet with one foot."

"I have bathed before."

Thekla pictures her raising the washcloth to her neck. Washing behind her ears. Down her shoulders. She wonders what it would be like to come here again, bring the gifts she has collected. But it feels wrong—in this forever of losing Bruno—to hope for her teacher to love her again. *The christening, Bruno, I can go to when I get to hold you at your christening, your tiny face already* altklug—*old-wise above the white lace gown, prayers and champagne—*

"You said you had one more question?" Sonja Siderova's voice. From the other side of the door.

—holy water on your downy scalp, Bruno, every moment happening at once, back and forth, every moment you have lived—the rosewood chess set that's yours alone, the punch of your chess clock, and "Schachmatt—*Checkmate," the battle cry of a brainy boy.*

Thekla feels herself reeling with despair. *I thought I was good for you, Bruno. But I'm no longer who I believed I was.*

The water is running again. Thekla imagines Sonja Siderova reaching up with her toes and maneuvering the faucets.

"I can't hear what you're saying, Thekla."

"I . . . didn't say anything."

"You had a question."

"Frau Abramowitz—is that why she disliked me so? Because of him?"

"Ilse did not dislike you."

"Did he ever think of leaving her? To be with my mother?"

"I can't answer that."

"If he had married my mother, I would have grown up in his house."

"You did grow up in his house."

Thekla draws a sharp breath. "What are you saying?"

"Ilse tried to adopt you."

*

"When Almut became pregnant with you," Sonja Siderova says, "Ilse wanted to bring you up as hers."

"Just Ilse?"

"You have to understand how much she wanted to be a mother. She was very young, but in four years of marriage she hadn't become pregnant, and she'd convinced herself she was barren. It was her sorrow. And this child to be was Michel's . . ."

Me— Thekla braces herself against the wall, slides down till she sits on the floor, legs splayed.

" . . . and Ilse wanted Michel's child. She paid for your mother's care, chose a home for unwed mothers by the Nordsee. It had an excellent doctor and was eight hours by train from Burgdorf. She took over in such a capable way that your mother was relieved to let her and agreed to the adoption. No one was to know. To have a child without marriage would have made your mother an outcast. You, too. In the meantime, Ilse pretended to be pregnant so that once the child—you—was born, no one in Burgdorf would suspect. Thekla?"

Thekla nods.

"Are you still there?"

Thekla nods.

Steam billows from the open door, and from that steam Sonja Siderova emerges, a towel clasped in front of herself. "I'm here." White foam makes her hair stand up in one peak. A horn.

Thekla used to twirl the soapy ends of her little brothers' hair into horns. They'd giggle, together in the tub, while Thekla would help *Mutti* wash their hair. Elmar and Dietrich. *Wilhelm Jansen's sons. Not Michel Abramowitz's.* So that's why Frau Brocker looked after them while Thekla was at the Abramowitzes'.

You did grow up in his house.

"How about him?" Thekla asks.

"Michel?" Sonja kneels next to Thekla, water dripping from her.

"Michel."

"He didn't know what to make of Ilse's . . . involvement. He held back. Watched. So unlike him. After Almut left, Ilse wanted him to tell his friends she was pregnant. But he refused. That's when she forced him by strapping on a pregnancy."

*

A rushing in Thekla's ears, almost like water, but it's not water, it's the telling, and in the telling her life is changing though it was always like this, except she didn't know. In the telling, she sees Sonja and Ilse stuff two pillowcases, one with the tight roundedness of early pregnancy, the other larger to overlay that roundedness. To each pouch they sew straps that hold the pregnancy in place, and Ilse parades that little belly through the neighborhood, smiles when people glance at it, then tells them she's expecting. Still, Michel won't tell anyone.

Ilse adds more padding until he either has to go along or expose her lie and his infidelity. The way he solves it is by letting it be known his child will be born in the fall.

One month before the birth, Ilse's belly slips during her early morning walk, and Sonja rushes her inside St. Martin's, where the stone walls and floors release the smell of centuries of incense. Crouching in a pew, Sonja adjusts Ilse's pouches. Half an hour before mass, and the other pews are still empty; but it's impossible to hide from the plaster saints who witness everything from their pedestals, St. Stefan and St. Agnes and St. Peter, their painted expressions forever scandalized.

Sonja points to them. "And what's worse than your striptease for the saints is that we're on the men's side of the church."

Ilse giggles. "Is that a sin here?"

"A near occasion of sin."

"I've never been inside a Catholic church." Ilse strokes the front of her navy blue dress. "The strangest thing is that I'm loving this . . . this thing that's to become my child. Can one love a pillow?"

"Depends on what kind of pillow," Sonja tries to joke.

"I used to worry that I'd forget to strap it on. Now I don't take it off while I sleep. Michel pretends not to notice. . . . Do you ever think his affair was meant to be?"

"Of course not."

"I do."

Sonja winces.

"Because of our child."

When they get to Ilse's house, a letter from Nordstrand is waiting. Sender: Almut Jansen. Not Almut Bechtel. Until now, the only letters from Nordstrand have come from Almut's doctor, who sends his reports to Ilse twice a month.

I was married to Wilhelm Jansen last Sunday, Almut writes. *My husband and I will raise our child together. I thank you for all you have done for us.*

"But she promised," Ilse cries.

"It is her child," Michel reminds her.

"Yours, too. That's why you don't want her to come back here."

"You must be respectful and leave her alone."

"You didn't leave her alone."

"Ilse—"

"She promised me the baby!"

"She's a married woman now." Awkwardly, he motions to her middle. "It's best to take that . . . that thing off."

"No." Ilse hugs both arms around herself. "I need to hear it from Almut."

"She has told you," he says gently, "in writing."

*

Sonja is the one who travels with Ilse to Nordstrand. Not Michel. Sonja doesn't want to. But she can't let her friend make that long trip alone. Fistfuls of white clouds rush in the opposite direction of their train. Swarms of red and yellow leaves. It's October. In the compartment, the two women sit next to one another. Ilse's face is pinched with fear; yet, in her voice is a hope that has nothing to do with Almut's decision to keep her baby. And that hope makes Sonja ache for her friend, who has traded her high spirits and humor for this fixation on a child that isn't hers, who believes that—if only she can get to Nordstrand before Almut gives birth, before Almut touches the child—she can hold Almut to her promise.

As the train nears Nordstrand, endless fields flit past their window, meadows edged by dikes, stone houses with roofs made from thick layers of grasses or from clay tiles. Thekla doesn't want the telling to stop. She knows this landscape well—not from her first year of life but from summers of visiting her grandmother. And in that landscape, Thekla sees her high-pregnant mother facing Ilse Abramowitz, whose strapped-on pregnancy is slack in comparison, their silhouettes like cutouts against the pale light cast off the tidal flats.

"The pillow child . . . ," Thekla whispers. "Not even real."

Chapter 37

THE CHILD WHO was you," Sonja says. "Come now, let's get you off the floor."

But when Thekla tries to stand, her legs give out.

"You want to hold on to me?" In Sonja's damp hair, the foam has grown porous, lacy.

"In a few minutes." Thekla touches her teacher's bare shoulder. The skin has dried but still smells of vanilla and rosewater, and Thekla is grateful that she does not pull away.

"Ilse kept hoping your mother would let her adopt you. But of course, your mother wouldn't. On the train back, Ilse curled into her seat and wept. Just before we reached Burgdorf, she tore off her pregnancy."

"What did she do with it?"

"Left it behind."

"On the train."

"Yes."

Thekla nods. "Make sure to rinse your hair."

"What?"

"It'll itch if you let it dry with soap in it."

*

"When you were three months old, Ilse and I returned to Nordstrand. By then, your mother worked in a stonecutter's house. We arrived on a Friday, but we couldn't visit you until Sunday, Almut's afternoon off. As soon as she let us in, Ilse handed me Michel's camera and reached for you." Sonja closes her eyes for an instant. "Ilse longed to touch you. So futile . . . and sad because it was obvious how strongly your mother loved you. When she finally let Ilse hold you, I took a photo."

"Tilted? Out of focus?"

"I didn't know how to use the camera properly. The photo cut off Ilse's hat but left so much floor that her feet seemed to be floating."

"So it's me she's holding."

"You've seen the photo?"

"What was I like?"

"Inquisitive. You studied us. You didn't suck your fingers or thumb like most babies. You had a lot of brown hair."

"Michel's coloring. How much did my father— How much did Wilhelm Jansen know?"

"He knew."

Falling then, Wilhelm, falling away from me again faster and getting smaller and smaller and falling and water in his mouth and his history in my bones, Wilhelm, an infant now, falling and almost drowning, forever. No longer my father? But then how come I still feel him in my bones, his falling and his love? I miss you, Vati—

"Does everyone know?" Thekla asks.

"No. Sister Josefine could not have hired you."

"But some gossiped."

"Some always gossip."

*

"You were almost a year old when Ilse disappeared. She hadn't mentioned you in months, but I knew where to find her. Michel and I went after her. He drove. When we got to Nordstrand, your mother and Ilse had made a pact, the old priest their witness: Ilse would not ask again about adopting you, and Almut would be the Abramowitzes' housekeeper and have you with her all day."

"Frau Abramowitz would have me with her, too."

"That was understood. Also that Ilse would make it possible for you to afford university."

"Even there . . . How much of my life did she not maneuver?"

"Your family could not have given you that education."

"And Michel?"

"Cautious. At first Michel was very cautious. But what could he do? We all drove back together, crowded into his car, you on Wilhelm Jansen's knees, your face to the window. A day's drive, but you barely slept, startled yourself awake whenever you got sleepy. You wanted to see everything. In Burgdorf, Michel spoke to Alexander Sturm about Wilhelm's skill as a toymaker. And Michel's mother, she took to you. She enjoyed reading to you, even when you were too little to sit on your own."

"I don't remember her."

"Judith Abramowitz. She lived with them. Actually, the house belonged to her. An extraordinary woman, someone who read Greek but let chickens into her house. During her final illness, Michel would bring you into her room, let you play on her bed, books all around you. You were her only grandchild when she died. Ruth and Albert weren't born yet."

*

"I'm still trying to take in that I'm related to them."

"To the same degree as you're related to Elmar and Dietrich. One parent."

Thekla nods.

"Gradually, Ilse and your mother came to like one another."

The instant Thekla says, "Not really," she remembers *Mutti* and Frau Abramowitz laughing together.

"What is it?"

"Once, *Mutti* was trying to sew on a button that had fallen off her blouse, but without taking off her blouse, and Frau Abramowitz was teasing, and they were both laughing and saying '*Wer sich das Zeug am Leibe flickt, der hat den ganzen Tag nicht Glück*—if you darn the clothes on your body, you won't have luck all day.' Then Frau Abramowitz took the needle and the button from *Mutti* and sewed it on for her."

"That comradery was there between them."

"Sometimes."

"When they did some project together. Still, it must have been hard for your mother to be working while Ilse read and played with you. Your mother wanted that . . . refinement for you, but she may have thought it would be more equal with her and Ilse."

"How could it be? She still was the one they paid, the one who washed their clothes and sheets."

"Yes, but it was difficult for Ilse, too. She didn't dare show any affection for you when your mother was in the same room. That photo of Ilse holding you, where did you—?"

"In the lining of *Mutti*'s sewing basket."

"Ilse was right, then, about Almut taking it because she didn't want Ilse to have even that little of you. It went missing the week after she returned to work for the Abramowitzes. Until Ilse had her own children, she was sure your mother would get jealous and take you away."

"And I believed her smile muscles were broken."

Sonja Siderova considers that. Touches her lips and smiles. "Last time I taught my anatomy lesson, there was no such muscle."

*

"When you became my teacher, I was afraid you wouldn't like me."

"Why?"

"Because she was your friend, and she didn't like me. I used to think it was because of the grapes." To say it aloud summons that familiar shame: *What have I done wrong?*

"Grapes?"

"I ate all her grapes. She called me greedy. Greedy like my mother. And that he, Michel, liked it . . . that greed in her."

"Ilse's love for you was . . . a complicated love. People said you brought her good luck, that when she became pregnant, it was from having you in the house."

Thekla has to smile. "That's beyond immaculate conception."

"Far beyond. Supposedly, you stirred up her mothering instincts. But as soon as Ruth was born, Ilse weaned herself from you. Abruptly. You didn't like it one bit. Stomped your feet. Clung to her."

"I don't remember."

"You've never forgiven her for that."

"What I do remember is how she was constantly at me about proper manners."

"You did love her, as a small child."

Chapter 38

IT WAS EASIER with Michel. He was kind to me. Always."

"Once he started to see himself in you—his quick mind, his own laughter—he wanted to give you whatever was his. He told me you enchanted him. But he also liked the . . . call it anguish of not being with you all the time."

Thekla tries to take that in.

"For him—" Sonja Siderova stops. "I think for him, love was too easy with the children he could openly name as his own."

"Once I was playing in front of our school, and he was across the street, about to go into the synagogue. When he saw me, he waited, asked if I wanted to come along. I ran to him. He took my hand in his. . . ." Thekla is back inside the synagogue with him, one hand against a marble pillar, not cold like marble in her church, just wood painted to look like marble. But the light is like the light inside her church because of the stained-glass windows. "Jerusalem," Herr Abramowitz says and points to the front. "That's where Jerusalem is." She nods, wants him to be proud of how much she knows about Jerusalem, tells him that's where the Jews crucified Jesus. But he puckers his lips together as if tasting something bad. "Let me show you something beautiful," he says, cups the top of her hair, gently, and leads her into the most beautiful library she's seen, old books and scrolls and tables. "A house of study and a house of prayer," he tells her. "You belong here, too."

You belong here, too. Knowing. The familiar warmth. And expecting him to be there. *He was always there.* She's overcome by an urgency to see him, have him tell her— *Tell me what? What I already know? That he thinks of me as his daughter? I want to hear him say it. Am terrified to hear him say it.*

Thekla is reeling with uncertainty. Only last year Fräulein Siderova was taking her students on hikes. But now she's not allowed to teach. Because she is Jewish. And soon Thekla will no longer be teaching. If she lets it be known that— That Herr Abramowitz is her father.

—*Nein nein jetzt nicht. Weg damit*—No no not now. Away with this—

But it's all unraveling, and she can't breathe.

How dare they? Isolate us first and then persecute us?

"Markus's parents understood the danger," she whispers.

Sonja nods.

"It'll get worse, right?"

"Each indignity made possible by the previous one."

"The one I keep thinking about is my—is Michel Abramowitz . . . and if he's safe."

"How far are you with your *Ahnenpass*?"

"I need two more documents."

"Get them. Fast. Get Wilhelm Jansen down on the line for father."

"He is on my birth certificate. Except the date is wrong, October instead of January."

"You were born in October."

"What?"

*

"When Almut moved back to Burgdorf, you were starting to walk. To make the numbers fit, she told everyone you were eight months old, that she'd married the toymaker the spring she moved to Nordstrand, and that you were born the following January."

"She said someone made a mistake."

"Someone sure did," Sonja blurts.

"I was told how I walked early . . . how well coordinated I was for my age. Except it wasn't my age."

"But that's how you've thought about yourself all along."

"Yes," Thekla says, surprised.

"Use your valuable Aryan ancestors. I would. If I had them."

"No reason to make it public now . . . about Michel Abramowitz."

"Absolutely not," Sonja says urgently. "Promise me—no heroics. Too dangerous."

"*Public* is the wrong word. It's not—"

"Listen to me, the *Ahnenpass* is not an ethical document. It forces disclosure to an unethical government."

"I mean open, not public. Open between him and me."

"Wait until being his daughter is no longer a threat to you."

"But I want to see him. Make sure he's safe."

"What can you possibly do to protect him?"

"I— I don't know yet."

"There's nothing."

Thekla blinks.

"The ones you can protect are our boys. But only if you protect yourself. Remind yourself what you're willing to do to teach. You've already proven that."

"I'm sorry." Thekla brings one hand to her throat. "What should

I have said when Sister Josefine came to me? Would you have wanted me to refuse?"

"Yes," Sonja says. "No." Her chin puckers. "I don't know."

"I have been so afraid to come to you. Can we talk again . . . like this? Please?"

No answer.

"If Sister Josefine figures this out— If people put it all together—" Thekla shakes her head. "So I'm suddenly Jewish at thirty-four?"

Sonja laughs aloud. "You're coming to it so late. That must count for something."

*

When Sonja stops laughing, she says, "We'll talk about our boys. We'll have to." She reaches across and touches Thekla's wrist.

It's a gesture of such unfathomable comfort that Thekla's eyes fill with tears. Then, that smell again, chalk and of sleep. *Soon, bones only. Oh, Bruno— Standing alone in the school yard, pretending not to notice the boys who're taunting you. Knocking at my door and hiding till I pick you up, swirl you around. Because of your long limbs, I assume you'll be almost weightless, but you're surprisingly solid in my arms as I swirl you—*

And in this swirl it's all happening at once and forever— Bruno suffocating inside the chess wardrobe, Marinus walking toward the guillotine, Jochen longing to be a hero, Schiller's diver getting crushed by the sea, Markus fleeing to America—and Thekla, too, is sucked into that vortex, Ilse's lost child, and though it's the past and she cannot change the past and has seen her moral courage for the frail thing it has become, that courage now flares up within her.

No more—

No more.

What seemed so benevolent at first—equality and community and employment for everyone—turned out to be lies that the Führer slipped into schools and homes, seducing and warping, until the people believed they were choosing for themselves; and out of this, they fabricated tales that were more distorted than mismatched fairy-tale blocks, more bizarre than any toymaker would have invented.

*

In the hallway window, that splinter of moon. Come dawn, it may still be visible when her boys walk to school. How much of her teaching has led them toward Schiller's cliff, toward the orders of a mad leader? When she left out the stanzas about the young diver's death, it was to shield her boys. Instead, she left out the danger beneath the surface. What if it's too late to make up what she kept from them?

No more.

Tomorrow she must warn her boys about the diver's second leap. That poem should not be listed under "courage" in the Echtermeyer. "Hubris" would be a more accurate heading. Fate may exalt you once, but to mistake that for allegiance and expect it again is arrogant. In too many poems that quest for heroism leads to death. Take Strachwitz's *"Das Herz von Douglas,"* when the crusader's heart is pierced by the lance of a pagan. Or Fontane's "John Maynard," where it's death by water and death by fire. How many ways can one body die?

Tomorrow she'll get to school early, write Schiller's missing stanzas on the chalkboard. When her boys arrive, they'll copy the stanzas, recite them together. That's how she'll begin. But the day after tomorrow, she'll introduce doubt into the diver's eagerness, encourage her boys to talk about different endings to the poem. What if the young diver had not stepped toward the mad king? What if he had not leapt into the rough waters? By imagining themselves as the diver, they'll unmask loyalty, glory.

She'll bring her boys through this, remind them that they, too, know what it is like to listen to tales around the flames, shivering, seeking even larger scares—creatures, colossal and primitive—that surpass all you've ever known. How you shift closer to one another, lean toward the flames, your feet hot, and reach with your sticks to turn the potatoes you've rolled into the fire, while you tell stories about a nebulous creature that takes on body to chase your souls. And yet, this is the kind of beast you can let near because you know—so deeply it lies beyond your earliest memories—that any beast you conjure cannot abscond with you. It's something your ancestors must have felt: to drive out the beast, you must first give it body, for all of you to see and fear and laugh at until you fathom what you truly are afraid of.